Merry Christmas Whiskey

A Whiskey Salvation Christmas Novella

Merry Christmas Whiskey

A Whiskey Salvation Christmas Novella

Chrissy Hartmann

Prickle Forrest Books
Published in Wooster, OH USA

COPYRIGHT

This is a work of fiction. Names, characters, places, and incidents either are the product of the author's imagination or are used fictitiously. Any resemblance to actual persons, living or dead, events, or locales is entirely coincidental.

Copyright © 2025 by
Chrissy Hartmann

All rights reserved. No part of this book may be reproduced or used in any manner without written permission of the copyright owner except for the use of quotations in a book review. For more information, address:
chrissyhartmann@sssnet.com

1st Edition November 2025

Cover designer *Getcovers*
Editing by *Cary Harter*

Library of Congress Control Number:
2025923308
ISBN (paperback): 978-1-965780-18-3
ISBN (eBook): 978-1-965780-19-0
ISBN (Large Print)

Published in Wooster, Ohio USA

www.chryissyhartmann.com

DEDICATION

For those whose holiday hearth is channeling a reindeer rodeo instead of quiet sparkle — amid the elf-wrapping marathons, rogue ribbons, and cheery chaos — may you find warmth not just in lights and bows, but in hope, healing, and the kind of new beginnings or second chances the mayhem can't steal.

Contents

Acknowledgements

Thanks a heap to all the brave couples who told me about their own *Merry Christmas Whiskey* moments — the ones where you dug deep for a second chance with the one you love, pulled on your boots, and raised your glass anyway. Your real-life chaos made this story richer than a Christmas pudding.

A holler of appreciation goes out to the ladies of the Wayne Novelist Guild — Cary, Cyndi, Ruth, Linda, Patricia, Judy, and Amanda — who helped brainstorm every last flurry of Christmas chaos. You turned "What if the reindeer ran off?" into "What if the cowboy shows up at the Antiquers Christmas tea wearing spurs?" and for that I'm forever grateful.

To my guy friends who bravely voiced their opinions on how one cowboy might *truly* handle these situations: I won't mention your names because yes, I'm aware someone might tease you for reading "holiday romances", but thank you for sticking your necks out and letting me borrow your voice.

To my son, Jacob — thank you for helping get the right Christmas vibe for the cover. Your sharp eye and "Mom, maybe the tree should lean a little" were worth every late night hot cocoa bull session.

To Mom and Dad — though you've long since taken separate trails, your dedication taught me that family needs to stick together through good times and bad. Thanks for reminding me what home means.

To my editor, Cary Harter — through your own Christmas chaos you set my sleigh on the right path and got this novella flying. I couldn't have landed this story without your steady hand and sharp edits.

To my husband — without your constant support and gentle reminders of our own jingle-bell chaos, I'd might have lost the reins. Thanks for keeping the bells ringing and believing in this dream from the start.

And finally, to God — without the birth of Your Son, none of this would be possible. Your love, grace, and holiday hope are the greatest gifts of all.

Love to you all, for staying by my side and continuing to ride this wild, wonderful snowy trail of storytelling together.

Chrissy Hartmann

Chapter 1

December 10th
San Antonio buzzed outside the windows of the Stapleton Event Coordinator's office. A light dusting of snowflakes danced in the air. Alexis Stapleton stared at the stack of invoices on her desk, but her mind wandered far from wedding cake samples and venue contracts.

Only fourteen more days until Christmas. Should I spend it here?

Her brow wrinkled causing a frown to pull at the corners of her mouth.

Or should I go home?

Her gaze wandered to a metal heart-shaped picture frame that sat next to a plate of candy cane cheesecake cookies on a snowman platter. There peeking out from it stood a gruffy looking cowboy with sawdust in his dark-brown hair holding a hammer. Her heart gave a wild thump almost as if prodding her to make up her mind.

Two weeks. Two weeks to decide.
She patted her chest.
Hold on, would you?
A soft knock at her door jerked her back to reality.

A reindeer poked its antlered head inside. "Morning, Mrs. Stapleton!" Lowell, the building's maintenance supervisor, stood in the doorway in a full reindeer suit, right down to jingling bells on his collar. He held a bright red envelope in his gloved hand. "Certified mail. Looks important."

Important? Probably nothing good.

Alexis' eyes zeroed in on the letter. Certified mail rarely brought good news. Ignoring the ridiculous costume for a moment, she reached out, catching a whiff of holiday cookies and floor polish as Lowell came closer. She plastered on a polite smile. "Thanks, Lowell. Guess Santa needs extra help around here?" She lifted an eyebrow trying to play along with the absurdity.

He grinned wide, showing off his dimples. "Management thought the costume would 'brighten the place up.' You think it's working?" He tossed in a wink.

A wink that Alexis did her best to sidestep.

Flirty.

Not the first time Lowell had been overly friendly since she and Brett split.

Alexis slid the envelope between her fingers, flipping it over to see a name. Just one name, though. A judge's name. And the judge's name appeared stamped across the back. Her heart dropped.

Divorce papers. Again.

Her stomach knotted, but she kept her expression neutral. "Well, it's definitely ... festive."

Lowell laughed, a deep, rich sound that echoed in the small office space. His eyes lingered on her just a bit too long before he gestured at the letter. "Might want to open that, though. Could be something you've been waiting on."

Waiting? Hardly. She wasn't ready to deal with it — whatever it was. Maybe not today. Maybe not ever. But, as always, curiosity got the better of her. She slid her finger under the flap, tore it open, and pulled out the crisp white papers. Her heart thudded. "Lowell, you mind giving me a minute?" Her tone came out lighter than she intended, but firm enough to get the message across.

The reindeer stepped back, but paused licking his lips. Then stepped toward her desk again. He pointed. "Uhh? Are those cookies the same ones you broght to the Christmas party last year?"

Alexis' Gaze followed the reindeer's finger, which pointed to a colorful decorated snowman platter. Her lips tugged upward. "They are."

He cleared his throat. One eyebrow rose. "Do you mind?"

Alexis laughed. ", would you like one?"

The reindeer leaned forward and took one. "These are my favorite."

Pink dotted Alexis' cheeks as the memory of her husband making that same statement as he ate a plateful the last Christmas they spent together filled her head. They were a simple cream cheese cookie and could be made with almost any flavor added, but the one everyone seemed to like the best were those made with the candy canes. And that included her husband.

The reindeer bells jingled,

She broke from her thoughts. "I'm glad you like them."

Lowell snagged another cookie. He pivoted with a smile as he raised the second cookie to his lips and jingled his way into the hall. "Holler if you need anything. Even Santa can use a helper."

When the door clicked shut, Alexis released the breath she hadn't realized she'd been holding. The office felt colder, quieter without the jingling bells, and suddenly, her hands shook as she unfolded the paper. The judge's neat handwriting filled the page, as though it wasn't enough to simply print out whatever this was.

Summons to Appear — her name printed in bold across the top. Her pulse quickened. Summoned? For what? It should've been over. She and Brett had already agreed to everything, hadn't they?

The next lines made her back stiffen. The judge requested her appearance to discuss "a final stipulation" before granting the divorce.

A stipulation?

Her brows rose.

What kind of stipulation?

Her mind raced, images of courtroom drama flooding her thoughts. Had Brett changed his mind? Did he want to contest something now? *Fight for more dates with the time share? Or worse — could this be about my business?*

Alexis groaned, pressing her fingers to her temples. Her life felt like a messy puzzle, each piece more frustrating than the last. At least at work, she could bury herself in tasks that required no emotion. No awkward conversations. No painful reminders that her marriage — the one she'd fought so hard for — had now come to its end.

The reindeer knocked again. "Alexis, I didn't mean to eavesdrop, but you look like you could use a coffee." Lowell popped his head back in, this time holding a mug shaped like Santa's boot. "Maybe something stronger?" His eyes sparkled with mischief.

Tempting. Not him. No.

Lowell wasn't the problem. Alexis missed ... something. Not Lowell's easy smiles or the way he never seemed to take life too seriously, but something familiar. Something — or someone — who grounded her in a way no one else ever had.

Her gaze dropped to the papers crinkled in her grip.

Brett.

Alexis shook her head and pushed the thought away. "I'm fine, really. Thanks, though."

Lowell shrugged, leaning against the doorframe like a reindeer on a smoke break. "You sure? You look like you've got a lot on your mind."

More than you know.

"I'm just... distracted, that's all."

"Distracted is one thing. Looking like you've seen a ghost is another." He nodded toward the letter in her hand. "Bad news?"

"Not exactly." Alexis bit her lip, folding the papers into neat thirds. "Just unexpected."

Lowell nodded, sympathy creeping into his eyes. "If you ever need to talk... or grab a drink, you know where to find me."

Alexis stuffed the papers back into the red envelope. "Appreciate it, but I'm good. Really."

No drinks. No flirting. No distractions.

Lowell lingered for a moment longer, then jingled his way back into the hallway, leaving Alexis alone with the faint smell of cinnamon and the heavy weight of her thoughts.

Divorce.

Even the word tasted bitter. She'd spent years trying to make things work with Brett. Five years of marriage, all based on teenage dreams and promises they'd made long before they knew how hard it would be to keep them. Her gaze drifted to the framed photo on her desk — the two of them at nineteen, laughing in front of a Ferris wheel, arms slung around each other like they were the only two people in the world.

Back then, everything had seemed so simple. Love had been enough, or at least that's what she'd believed. Brett had been her best friend, her rock. The one who could always pull her back when her wild energy started to spiral out of control. She sighed, rubbing her temples again. *It wasn't supposed to end like this.*

Her phone buzzed, pulling her back to the present. A text from her lawyer.

'Did you get the letter from the judge?' Need to discuss ASAP.

Of course, they did. What now?

Alexis tossed the phone aside and stood, stretching her stiff limbs. Work. She needed to throw herself into something productive, anything to keep her mind off the mess that her life had become. But the letter loomed over her like a dark cloud, refusing to be ignored.

She couldn't stop thinking about it — the stipulation. One more thing before it's all over. One more thing before she and Brett could finally close this chapter. But deep down, she wasn't sure she wanted it to be over. Not really.

Maybe that's why Lowell's flirty smile hadn't fazed her. Not because she wasn't tempted by the easy distraction he offered, but because she only wanted one person to walk through that door — Brett.

But it wouldn't happen. Not now, not ever.

Chrissy Hartmann

FROM: The Whiskey Tattler Editors
TO: Whiskey Tattler Subscribers
CC:
Date: December 10th 3:04 pm CST
Subject: Lover or candy cane? You pick ...

The Whiskey Tattler

Feature Editorial: Love is for Suckers and Candy Canes
A twin editorial. Hazel wrote it. Harriet fixed it.

By Hazel Montgomery
Let's just say it plain: love is a seasonal illusion best paired with fudge and ignored by anyone over fifty. It starts with shared hot cocoa and ends with a separate lawyer.
Just look at Alexis and Brett Stapleton. One minute they're high school sweethearts, next minute they're playing Claus and filing paperwork. The moral? Stick to pets. Or potted plants. They don't talk back.

Editor's Notes:
By Harriet Montgomery
Now, now. Not everyone ends in disaster, though 76% of December couples in this town do, according to our informal study and three rounds of margaritas.
Still, there's something about Alexis' eyes when Brett makes her laugh. And we've both seen how he watches her when she's not looking. That ain't the look of a man ready to walk away.
But as Hazel points out ... That took place five years ago. Question Whiskey wants to know, Does Brett still have the resources to light her tree or is the frost permanent now?

So yes, love might be for suckers. But even the strongest peppermint stick can melt in hot cocoa. And this story ain't over.

Hazel and Harriet Montgomery
Twins - Tattlers - Truth-tellers and vortex busters

Chapter 2

December 11th

Brett Stapleton rubbed his temples and glared down at the piece of paper that had been haunting his workbench all morning. That fancy courthouse letterhead looked out of place amidst the sawdust and hand tools, like it had wandered in from another universe — divorce summons. Except in the 28 years of knowing Judge Henry, he wasn't the type to make anything easy. Brett didn't know what the old man had up his sleeve, but the note had 'not so fast' written all over it, at least that's how he interpreted it with the mention of additional stipulations. He frowned, tapping a finger on the page, feeling the tension coil tight in his chest. As if his life needed more complications.

The door to his workshop creaked open, letting in a gust of frigid air along with a sharp click of heels on the floorboards. Brett didn't bother looking up. Only one person in town would walk into his space like they owned it, and only one person would do it in heels.

"Brett Stapleton," came the smooth voice of Serena Foster, dripping with that polished professionalism she wielded like a hammer. "You look like you've swallowed a cactus."

Brett grunted, his green eyes lifting up at her briefly. She stood there, all tailored coat and perfectly styled hair, looking as out of place in his workshop as that summons. But didn't stop her from strolling right in like she belonged there. *Typical Serena.*

"I'm fine." He turned his attention back to the papers, willing her to take the hint and leave. But in all honesty, Serena never could take a hint. After all, Stapletons were a brood of their own, even if her branch of the tree had been stripped clean of its bark.

"Fine, huh?" She sidestepped a stack of wood, making her way to the bench, her gaze sharp and nosy. "That why I heard through the grapevine Judge Henry's got some plans for you?"

That got him. Brett's head shot up, eyes narrowing as he studied her. "You've been back to town a whole six months and you think you know everything that's been going on?"

Serena smiled as wide as the Rio Grande. "Social media, my dear cousin. You really should try it."

Brett scoffed as he crumpled the paper in his hand. Then glancing up he blew out his breath. "What'd you hear?"

Serena smirked, clearly enjoying his irritation. "Oh, just that your little divorce isn't gonna be the quick in-and-out you were hoping for." She tapped a finger against the wood he'd been sanding. Her nails looked like they belonged in a jewelry catalog, not his workshop. "Word is, Judge Henry's got some 'festive ideas' in mind. You'll have to work for that freedom of yours."

Brett's stomach twisted. He clenched his fists on the workbench, the worn wood grounding him for a second.

Work for it?

That old coot already made this hard enough with his cryptic letter.

What the hell did he mean by -festive ideas?

A deep, frustrated groan rumbled in his chest, but he kept it there, locked behind his clenched jaw.

"You've gotta be kidding me," he pushed the paper aside as if doing so would erase the whole mess.

"I wish.," Serena smiled wide uncomfortably cheerful for someone delivering the unwelcomed news. "But you know Judge Henry. He's not exactly the -sign here and move along- type."

The blood pounded in Brett's ears. Judge Henry wasn't a man who played fair. He liked to watch people squirm, enjoyed the spectacle. The thought of jumping through hoops to get his divorce grated against every nerve in his body. He rubbed the back of his neck. The frustration bubbled up. "What the hell kind of game is this?"

Serena shrugged, but the amusement never left her eyes. "Some kind of Christmas challenge, from what I hear. Twelve tasks. Twelve deeds. Before Christmas."

Twelve deeds?

His eyes widened as a strange mix of disbelief and anger sparked inside him. "For a divorce?"

"Yup. Seems like old Judge Henry has been watching too many holiday movies." She glanced at him, her voice dropping slightly. "He's making you and Alexis work for it."

The mention of Alexis, his soon-to-be ex-wife, sent a jolt through his chest. They'd already done the work — or tried to, hadn't they? Well, Alexis had tried. She'd planned, talked, pushed for him to open up, but asking a fence post to dance would have been easier. His world had always been simple: work, home, quiet. Hers? The total opposite. Parties, people, plans. She thrived on connection. But not Brett. In fact, it suffocated him.

He shifted Uncomfortably under the weight of the memories. He'd married Alexis thinking they could balance each other out. Turns out, you can't tie down a firefly.

"I'm not doing this." The words shot out, more to himself than to Serena, though she didn't miss a beat.

"Oh, you'll do it," A quirk to one side of her lips appeared. "And you'll hate every second of it, but deep down, part of you probably won't mind too much."

Brett's eyes narrowed. "What's that supposed to mean?"

She crossed her arms, leaning against the workbench, one heel tapping against the floor with slow deliberation. "Let's not pretend you're in a rush to sign those papers. If you were, you'd have been on Judge Henry's doorstep yesterday. But here you are, still staring at that summons like it's a snake in your boot."

His gut twisted. Heat crept up the back of his neck. She wasn't wrong, but admitting that out loud? Not a chance. He crossed his arms over his chest, keeping his expression neutral. "I just don't like being jerked around."

"Uh-huh," Serena dragged out the word making him want to toss her right out the door. "Or maybe you're not so sure about the whole divorce thing.

Maybe there's a part of you — some tiny, stubborn, mule-headed part — that still thinks Alexis' worth fighting for."

Brett's jaw clenched. Alexis portrayed everything he didn't — bright, social, full of energy. And that had been great once, back when they first got together. He'd loved how she could walk into a room and make everyone laugh. And how her laugh had this contagious ripple to it. But that — well, it got exhausting. He hadn't been made for her world, and his... well it didn't satisfy her.

But maybe Serena had a point. Maybe some part of him, buried deep under all the frustration and distance, still wanted to hold onto Alexis, even if the smart thing to do would be to let her go.

A bitter laugh escaped before he could stop it. "You think Judge Henry's Christmas game is gonna fix all that?"

Serena smiled, a softer one this time, as if she could see the cracks he tried to hide. "Maybe not. But it might make you realize what you actually want."

He chuckled again, this time more at himself than the situation. "And what if I don't even know what that is?"

"Well," she pushed off the workbench and smoothed out her coat, "that's what Judge Henry's game is for. You've got twelve tasks to figure it out, Cowboy."

Brett watched her. His amusement faded into something closer to confusion. The old Brett — the one who'd carved his life from wood and silence — would've been furious. Would've stormed over to Judge Henry's office and demanded an explanation. But now? He didn't know what to feel. Somewhere in that mix of anger and uncertainty, a flicker of something else, something that almost felt like hope waited.

Serena's heels clicked again as she moved toward the door, her parting words floated back to him with a grin he couldn't see but could definitely hear. "Good luck... You're gonna need it."

The door swung shut, leaving Brett alone with the soft hum of the wind outside and the distant creak of the old barn. His gaze drifted back to the divorce papers, Judge Henry's cryptic message glaring up at him. Twelve deeds.

He rubbed his jaw.

Maybe, just maybe, I need this.

He raked a hand through his hair.

Not to win Alexis back, but to figure out if I even want to.

He picked up the hammer, turning it over in his hands. The weight of it felt familiar, comforting. He'd spent years building things — solid, lasting things. But when it came to building a life with Alexis? He'd somehow managed to use the wrong tools.

"Hmm? Twelve deeds."

FROM: The Whiskey Tattler Editors
TO: Whiskey Tattler Subscribers
CC:
Date: December 11th 4:03 pm CST
Subject: Divorced in December

The Whiskey Tattler

Where Are They Now? Divorced in December Edition

By Hazel and Harriet Montgomery

A cautionary tale with a little peppermint on top.
Once upon a time in Whiskey, December was the month for snow, sentiment, and surprisingly hostile breakups.

We've compiled a brief-but-brutal rundown of former hometown couples who called it quits during the holidays. Why? For perspective. And because we're a public service, darling.

The December Downfalls:
• Bobby Joe and Tammy-Lynn (2013)
Split after the infamous Candy Cane Parade Float Fiasco. She threw a peppermint stick at his truck.
Current status: She married the float driver.

• Gina and Carlos (2016)
Tried to "rekindle things" by taking a holiday pottery class. Result: one cracked snowman and a restraining order.
Current status: She sells Etsy ornaments shaped like middle fingers.

• Marybeth and George (2019)
Lasted through Christmas Eve...until his mama brought up her ex over mashed potatoes.
Current status: Marybeth lives in Austin. Jake still eats alone at the diner.

• And now: Alexis and Brett:
Looks as if rumor's true. Got confirmation from the Whiskey Express mail service that Judge Henry's sent out not one, but two red envelopes, and no, they weren't for no Christmas cards either. So, is there possibility for a second chance? Public humiliation? Spontaneous re-proposal under the tree?

Chrissy Hartmann

Hazel bets five bucks on a Christmas Eve smooch. I on the other hand, say, Girl, double it!

Stay tuned as this holiday is just getting started and there's no place better to be than Whiskey!

EDITORS NOTE:
As for the rumor on the Barleyshot special edition they're putting out this year, we've been told it might be out a wee late, but that's not Jack's fault. After all, the man's not the 'all mighty', — Even, though he thinks he is.
And yes, he's promised one bottle of the special edition of their all too famous Cinnamon Whiskey will be available to each couple who attends the annual Whiskey Christmas Eve ball. So, get your tickets soon!

Hazel and Harriet Montgomery
Twins - Tattlers - Truth-tellers and Cinnamon Whiskey Sippers

Chapter 3

December 12th
Alexis sat in the stiff leather chair across from Judge Henry's desk, the smell of old paper and tobacco lingering in the air like an unwanted guest. The judge squinted at the stack of papers in front of him, adjusting his reading glasses as he hummed under his breath. Beside her, Brett leaned back casually in his chair, hat balanced on one knee, weathered brown boots crossed at the ankles. The contrast between them glared at her. Alexis' back remained rigid with arms tightly folded across her chest as though bracing for another fight.

Judge Henry, a solid man in his sixties, looked up from the paperwork, giving them both a look that had stopped more than one heated argument in its tracks over the years. "Divorce," he began, "As I've mentioned before, I'd hoped never to see the two of you in here for this particular conversation." He closed the folder with a snap that made Alexis flinch.

Across the room, a grandfather clock ticked loudly, each second feeling heavier than the last. The tension hung thick between Alexis and Brett, neither of them willing to speak first. Instead, Brett tapped the brim of his hat, glancing sideways at her with a look that carried more frustration than words could express. Alexis shifted in her seat, avoiding his gaze, determined to remain unfazed. She had come here to make this official, to move on.

Judge Henry cleared his throat, his silver-gray eyes twinkling with an unreadable expression. "Well, I ain't signing these divorce papers today." He pushed the stack of documents aside like they were nothing more than mailbox ads.

Her pulse quickened. "Excuse me?"

Brett turned toward the judge, brow raised but not exactly surprised.

Judge Henry leaned back in his chair, folding his hands over his round belly, enjoying the weight of his next words. "Not until you two do a little something for the town. Twelve somethings, actually."

Alexis blinked, her mind racing to catch up. "You can't be serious."

Judge Henry grinned, a mischievous gleam in his eye. "I'm dead serious, Miss Party Planner." IIis gaze shifted to Brett, who shifted in his seat, looking a bit too comfortable for Alexis' liking. "I've thought long and hard about this. What better way to make sure you two can actually live without each other than working together for a while? For the good of the town, of course."

Alexis groaned inwardly. This could not be happening.

Judge Henry leaned forward, pointing at the divorce papers like they might bite. "I'll sign these after you two complete twelve deeds for Christmas. One for each day until Christmas Eve."

Brett's shoulders shook with silent laughter.

Alexis shot him a glare sharp enough to cut wood.

He tipped his hat to her in response, that cocky grin she'd once found charming peeking out from behind his stubbled jaw and mustache now an infuriating reminder of why this whole thing started in the first place.

Judge Henry slapped his hands on his desk, his booming voice cutting through the tension like a bull at a rodeo. "This town's been good to both of you, and now it's your turn to be good to it. Deliver Christmas trees, wrap the secret santa gifts, help with the Christmas Eve dance — whatever the town needs, you two will handle it."

Alexis struggled to keep her breathing steady, biting back the urge to scream. She didn't have time for this. A party planner in San Antonio, with a holiday season packed to the brim with clients, deadlines, and expectations. But none of that seemed to matter in this little office that smelled like old leather and stubbornness. Brett's presence next to her didn't help. The man could fix anything — except their marriage, apparently.

Judge Henry glanced between them, raising an eyebrow. "Look, I'm not saying you'll fall back in love." His voice softened with something that might have been a trace of compassion, though Alexis wouldn't bet on it.

"But either you'll figure out that you still care about each other, or you'll know for certain this divorce is what you need." He leaned back again, as if the plan he'd concocted had no hitches with it. "Either way, the town gets its holiday spirit back, and I don't have to sign anything until you're sure."

Alexis' jaw clenched. "This is absurd."

Brett chuckled beside her, low and deep "Could be worse, darlin'. He could've made us decorate ornaments with a bunch of preschoolers."

Alexis rolled her eyes. "Not funny... In fact, it might be fun, Mr. Scrooge."

The judge leaned forward, pushing the divorce papers aside with a chuckle. "That's not a bad idea." He grabbed a pencil and scribbled on a piece of paper. After he set the pen down, he picked up the paper and shook it out. A long list unfurled. "Here's your first deed. Tomorrow, you'll be helping to finish up decorating the town square. Be there by nine sharp."

Alexis thought of the items the judge had just mentioned and groaned audibly. The tasks lined up like a parade of unwanted headaches. Decorating the square, bell hanging, Tree deliveries, secret santa gift wrapping. The list went on.

Oh lordy, he doesn't want us to do all these, right?

Brett leaned over and tapped the desk grinning. "Looks like we're gonna be real busy, partner."

Heat prickled the back of Alexis' neck.

This couldn't be happening. Twelve days of forced togetherness — twelve days of awkward silences, old arguments, and memories better left in the past.

Alexis' stomach sank, but her heart, well it did a little two step on its own.

Stop it. We're not going there.

Judge Henry waved them toward the door. "Go on now." He smiled with a twinkle in his eye. "I've got to finish my list." He held up the long slip of paper. "Get some rest. Tomorrow's a busy day. The town square won't decorate itself."

Chrissy Hartmann

FROM: The Whiskey Tattler Editors
TO: Whiskey Tattler Subscribers
CC:
Date: December 12ᵗʰ 5:07 pm CST
Subject: Let the Holiday Hijinks Begin…

THE WHISKEY TATTLER

Spreading Christmas cheer
one juicy tidbit at a time.

By: Hazel and Harriet Montgomery

Christmas deeds… or ways to off your ex?

According to a reliable source: "Judge Henry and his overpoured eggnog, the soon-to-be-maybe-not couple, Mrs. Alexis Stapleton and Mr. Brett Stapleton are required to complete twelve community-based Christmas deeds — together — before their divorce can be finalized."

Yes, together. Like, breathing the same air. Voluntarily. And they may even be required to do it in flannel, after all, Orange doesn't look good at this time of the year.
Apparently, signing on the dotted line ain't enough anymore. In the spirit of the season and possibly Judge Henry's senility, our beloved ex-sweethearts must spread cheer, decorate cookies for the Christmas Tea, deliver groceries to grumpy shut-ins, and generally not strangle each other under the mistletoe… Or something like that. We're all taking bets on who caves first.

Current Odds:
• Alexis leaves Brett in a snowdrift: 3 to 1
• Brett accidentally forgets to pick her up for Task number 4: 5 to 1
• Mistletoe kiss by Deed number 7: Even money
• They fall back in love and ruin our cynicism: 10 to 1 — ugh!

Let's be clear, dear readers: this isn't a Hallmark movie. This is Whiskey. We do things a little more… explosively around here.

We'll keep you all posted after each deed. In the meantime, pass the cocoa, hide the mistletoe, and for heaven's sake, someone warn the carolers.

Until the next scandal,

Hazel and Harriet Montgomery
Twins - Tattlers - Truth-tellers

Chrissy Hartmann

Chapter 4

December 13th

Brett leaned against his black truck with arms crossed, watching the town square buzz with holiday chaos. Strings of Christmas lights draped lazily across lampposts, barely clinging to their hooks. A ladder stood crooked by the Whiskey Salvation Shelter, threatening to topple over at the next gust of wind. People darted around like ants, hauling boxes of decorations, fixing wreaths, and trying to give the square a festive look before the big lighting ceremony later that night. Beans and Leaves had already set out their peppermint coffee specials, the smell wafting across the street and blending with the vanilla sweetness coming from Scoops. The cheery atmosphere around the ice cream shop drew customers to it no matter the weather. But something about the whole thing felt ... unfinished.

Brett glanced over at Alexis, who stood a few feet away, clipboard in hand, eyes darting around as if she were managing a corporate event rather than a small-town Christmas. She tapped one of her black sheik boots she always loved to wear, and Brett could practically hear the gears turning in her mind. Always so serious, so focused, even when they used to — well before everything got complicated.

Alexis frowned, narrowing her eyes at the lopsided wreath hanging over the door to Scoops. "That wreath is crooked." She marched over without another word, lifting her hand to fix it.

"Of course it is," Brett muttered under his breath, pushing off his truck and following her. "Pretty sure nobody cares, Alexis."

She ignored him, stretching on her toes to adjust the wreath's ribbon.

Brett caught a glimpse of her frustrated expression, and for a split second, amusement bubbled up inside him.

Always had to be perfect.

The wreath gave her trouble, hanging just out of her fingers reach.

He shook his head and stepped closer. Not wanting to throw her off balance, he stepped up behind her about a whisper away breath away, and extended one red and white flannel clad arm and the light swoosh of his puffy vest against her red jacket, he reached over her and straightened the wreath with one swift movement. "Better?"

Alexis growled just low enough for him to hear with her jawline tight. "I had it. You didn't need to —"

"You're welcome." He shot her a smile cutting her off, then turned his attention to the rest of the square.

More lights needed hanging, garland too, and that ladder still looked ready to send someone to the hospital.

Alexis crossed the street, the faint jingle of a bell rang out as someone pushed open the door to Beans and Leaves carrying a tray of steaming cups toward the volunteers. The smell reached Brett's nose. A sense of warmth and calm filled him — if only for a moment.

Alexis had her hands full with her clipboard again, eyes scanning the square as she made more notes, *probably plotting ways to fix what she saw as chaos.*

"What's next?"

Because she's always got something next.

Snowflakes began to fall. The temperature dropped another few degrees.

Alexis tugged on her red quilted jacket then brushed the few flurries from the clipboard. " The garland needs to go up around the Whiskey Salvation Shelter. And those candy canes need fixing." She nodded toward the large, red-and-white decorations sticking out of the ground at odd angles. "I also think the banner could be — "

"Garland first," Brett interrupted, already moving toward the box of tinsel shoved haphazardly against the curb. "One thing at a time."
The crisp scent of pine and cinnamon filled the air, but it did little to calm the tension crackling between them. Alexis might have a plan for every inch of this square, but Brett knew better than to let her run wild. Perfection wasn't the goal here, despite her belief that she might be held responsible.

He hauled the garland across the street in front of the shelter and started looping it around the posts on the sidewalk. His fingers worked it quickly through the loops. The green and gold crackled softly as it slipped through his hands. The movement grounded him, giving him something to focus on other than the silence between them.

Alexis hovered nearby, clearly itching to micromanage the process, but for once, she didn't say a word. Instead, she scribbled furiously on her clipboard.

"Judge Henry's gonna love this." Brett shook his head as he adjusted the last loop of garland. "He gets free labor, and we get stuck doing his dirty work."

Alexis finally glanced up from her notes, her brow furrowed. Her shoulders dropped as she let out a sigh. "He'll love it if it's done right."

Brett rolled his eyes but couldn't help the slight tug at the corner of his mouth. "Right. Which means it's gotta meet your standards, not just his."

Alexis didn't respond, but instead bristled. She pressed her lips together with arms folded as she glanced around the square once more searching for the next thing to fix.

The decorations sparkled under the morning light, casting a soft glow over the town, but Alexis still seemed dissatisfied.

"Gonna drive yourself crazy looking for flaws," Brett muttered as he tied off the last bit of garland. He stepped back, dusting his hands on his jeans, surveying the square. The scene looked festive enough. But an edge of something else crept in — maybe her presence, her focus on making everything perfect, or maybe the memory of how easily they used to tackle projects like this together.

Without missing a beat, Alexis walked over to the candy canes and kneeled down to straighten the ones sticking out at awkward angles. Her hands worked quickly, fixing what most people probably wouldn't even notice. She moved efficiently, barely sparing Brett a glance, though he could sense her frustration simmering beneath her calm exterior.

And with that cheshire cat grin of his he tried not to laugh. "Didn't realize crooked candy canes could ruin Christmas."

"They won't." She yanked another candy cane upright. "But they might ruin a perfectly good display."

Brett scratched his jaw, the scent of freshly brewed coffee drifting from Beans and Leaves again. "Perfect displays. Always with the perfection."

Alexis didn't answer, standing up and dusting off her hands before turning back to face him. For a second, her eyes met his, and the tension between them thickened.
Brett blinked first. Of course he did. Alexis had a way of looking straight through a man, slicing past pride and excuses like she was born with X-ray vision and a meat slicer.

She broke the silence with a sigh that came from somewhere deep — somewhere irritated. "We still have to finish the Christmas tree. Judge Henry will have a coronary if we leave it half-done."

The two-story blue spruce tree loomed in the middle of the square like it owned the damn place, branches fluffed with the aggression of someone taking out their anger on a loofah. Alexis stood beside it, hands on hips, jaw set tight. One string of lights draped over her shoulder like a badge of combat.

Brett cleared his throat. "You realize you've rearranged those same ornaments three times now, right?"

"Yeah? And you've stood there holding that star like you're auditioning for a perfume commercial. Are you gonna put it on the top or spit shine it?"

Brett squinted at the porcelain gold star in his hand. It glowed as if to put off a warning. Like it knew it was about to witness the collapse of a marriage and a twenty-foot tree. He walked to the base. "Didn't peg you for the bossy elf type."

Alexis climbed the ladder, dragging a strand of red beads with her. "That's because you never paid enough attention."

"Careful now," he drawled. "A man might take that as a jab."

She leaned out to reach the far branch, the hem of her red coat lifting just enough to reveal those damn jeans. The ones that had caused at least four arguments and a suspicious number of broken remote controls over the years.

He stepped closer, gaze reluctantly dragging from denim to her grip on the ladder. "You sure that thing's steady?"

"Worried about me, Cowboy?"

"No. Worried about the lawsuit I'd have to settle if your dramatic ass takes a swan dive into the nativity scene."

Alexis shifted her weight, the ladder creaked, just enough to yank his gut into a knot. The wind caught her long curly sable-colored hair, spun it like a country music video, and for one traitorous second, he didn't mind decorating a Christmas tree in the middle of downtown with his almost-ex-wife.

She stretched further. "I've got it — "

The ladder gave a soft lurch.

"Whoa — Alexis."

Then she fell. All red coat and flailing limbs and a yelp that sounded suspiciously like a curse.

Brett caught her. Barely. Her body slammed into his, knocking the breath out of both of them. They stumbled back a step, then two, until his boot hit the tree decoration that Alexis had dropped. And they landed with a thud in the snow.

Alexis blinked up at him, wide-eyed and half-laughing, her hand clutching the front of his jacket. Her breath came fast, her nose pink from the cold — or maybe the blush crawling up her cheeks.

"You always this handsy with holiday accidents?" Her voice low, almost too close.

He looked down at her, hair full of tinsel and pride looking about as bruised as his ribs. "Only with women who try to kill themselves via Christmas decor."

Again nothing. She just stared.

He opened his mouth to say something — anything to break the silence — but the sound of boots crunching over the snowy sidewalk interrupted the moment.

Judge Henry ambled into the square, his wide-brimmed hat casting a shadow over his face as he surveyed the decorations. His large hands rested on his waist. He took in the garland, the wreaths, the candy canes, and the tree.

With snowflakes and a few twigs from the Christmas tree clinging on to their coats, Brett stood with Alexis still in his arms, straightened, watching the judge's reaction closely. The man had a way of making even the simplest of tasks feel like life or death, but today, something about his expression looked... pleased.

"Well, well," Judge Henry drawled, squinting up at the tree they'd almost fixed. "Seems you all managed not to burn the town down yet." He glanced between the two. His smirk unmistakable. "Decorations look good enough... and the tree. Well, it will do."

Alexis straightened her clipboard, smoothing the pages as if she'd just finished the critique herself.

Brett stuffed his hands into his pockets, trying to suppress the smile tugging at the corners of his mouth.

Judge Henry grunted, stepping closer to inspect the Christmas tree. After a long pause, he nodded. "You all are clear to move on to your next deed after you get that star up there." He handed Alexis another piece of paper, his grin widened. "Old George McAlister's truck's broken down. You'll be delivering BIO block to his farm tomorrow. Man needs it to heat his cabin this winter, and since he can't haul it himself, that's where you two come in."

Brett raised an eyebrow, glancing at Alexis. "BIO block, huh?"

"Seems like more your area. " Alexis' lips twitched in the slightest of smiles.

He returned the smile. "Guess it's time to load up." But his gaze lingered on Alexis for a moment longer before he turned toward his truck, the question lingering in his mind.

Twelve good deeds, huh?

Still not crazy about all this, he massaged the back of his neck.

How many more of these are going to involve spending so much time with her. Bigger question, are we going to survive this without driving each other crazy?

FROM: The Whiskey Tattler Editors
TO: Whiskey Tattler Subscribers
CC:
Date: December 13th 5:07 pm CST
Subject: The Latest Happenings…

THE WHISKEY TATTLER

If it happens in Whiskey, we're already writing on it.
By Hazel and Harriet Montgomery
Deed Watch: Day Number One
Task: Decorating the Square

You can't make this stuff up, folks.
Yesterday at precisely 9:07 a.m. — because Alexis is always punctual and Brett is allergic to punctuality — our estranged couple arrived at the town square dragging boxes of ornaments and unresolved issues.

Alexis wore a red puffy coat with vengeance in her eyes. Brett wore flannel like it owed him money.
They were supposed to trim the town tree, hang the decorations, and "rekindle a sense of community spirit," as Judge Henry so poetically put it. What actually happened was:
• Two broken ornaments.
• One argument over candy cane placement.
• A ladder standoff (she climbed it, he held it, we prayed).
• And an awkward moment involving a fallen star topper and Brett catching Alexis by the waist.

Witness Statement:
a.k.a. Mildred at the bakery:
"They were bickering so loud I dropped my plateful of gingerbread. But then she laughed, y'all. I swear. She laughed. Like the cute, flirty kind. The world tilted."

Hazel's Verdict:
It was a giggle. Nothing counts unless it snorts.

Harriet's Counterpoint:
It was a pre-snort. Things are heating up.

Christmas Shoppers Overheard: Judge Henry stopped by mid-deed, grinned like he'd invented romance, and reminded them that if they skipped a task, he'd tack on three more. The man is a sadist in a Santa hat.

Final square rating: 7 out of 10
Final mood rating: Sassy with a side of simmering tension
Number of times Alexis rolled her eyes: Five.
Number of times Brett looked like he wanted to say something meaningful but choked on sarcasm instead: Three.
Number of witnesses hoping for a kiss under the town hall's mistletoe: Everyone but us (we were hoping for popcorn and a slap.)

Stay tuned for Day 2 where rumor has it, they'll be delivering bio block to old George McAlister's dressed as Mr. And Mrs. Claus. Maybe, but one can hope.

Naughty or Nice, we're on the job,

Hazel and Harriet Montgomery,

Twins, Editors of the Whiskey Tattler, and Christmas Tree Ornament Makers

Chapter 5

December 14th

Alexis sat stiffly in the passenger seat as Brett's truck rumbled up the dirt road leading to George McAlister's tree farm. The narrow path curved through thick rows of pine trees. Their branches heavy with the scent of Christmas. Each bump in the road jostled the Bio block in the truck bed, the boxes rattling together as if announcing their arrival. George's cabin appeared at the end of the trail, nestled among the trees like it had grown there naturally, weathered, but sturdy. The sight of the place brought an unexpected knot to Alexis' chest.

Beside her, Brett eased the truck to a stop, letting the engine idle for a moment before turning the key. He slid out of the driver's seat, boots hitting the ground with a thud. Alexis followed suit stepping down onto the gravel driveway.

An older gentleman pushed open the weathered door of the cabin. He waved from the top step of the porch where he stood. His face lit up as he waved at them with a hand on the railing for balance. The man's gray beard and worn-flannel shirt only added to the feeling that time had slowed down in this little corner of the world. "Y'all made it."

Brett smiled with a nod already rounding the truck to unload the first box. "Howdy, George."

Alexis watched him for a beat longer than necessary, then turned her attention back to George. "We brought the Bio block, just like the judge said."

George grinned over his shoulder as he pulled open the creaky porch door. "Come on inside for a minute. Let me give you all something to warm up before you start hauling all that."

Alexis followed George inside. The familiar smell of pine and wood smoke filled her nose as soon as she stepped over the threshold. The small cabin had an air of coziness to it, the kind of place where you couldn't help but feel at home. A fire crackled softly in the hearth casting flickering shadows on the walls lined with photos. Some were of George, younger, laughing beside his wife, others of his children and grans. An ache tugged at her as her gaze lingered on the images.

George headed toward his kitchen. "You and Brett remind me of me and my Sarah." He glanced over his shoulder with a smile. "She always stood by my side helping out with the farm, especially this time of year. Christmas trees, those blocks for the fire — she loved it all." He pointed at the wall where a framed photo of Sarah hung. His wife stood next to him with arm looped through his with a big smile.

Alexis didn't speak. Instead, she looked over her own shoulder at Brett who stood outside, lifting the first load of Bio block as if it weighed nothing. His broad back strained against his flannel shirt. Muscles shifting with each movement. They'd once worked together like that, side by side, tackling whatever life threw at them. The memory of that partnership stirred something deep within — an unsettling mix of emotions she hadn't planned on revisiting.

George chuckled as he came back to the living room with two steaming mugs. "You two ever work together before all this?" He handed one to her. His eyes twinkled with curiosity.

"Yes," Alexis took the mug from him. The heat seeped into her cold fingers as she wrapped her hands around the cup bringing it to her lips. The warmth spread through her chest, but it didn't quite chase away the confusion swirling inside her.

George smiled as if he had just figured out a secret. "It's nice to see. Reminds me of better times. Only a handful of folks can pull that off these days, you know."

She glanced at the doorway where Brett had just walked back inside for the next load. He paused for a second. His gaze met hers across the room. Her pulse quickened. The moment stretched longer than it should have. George's words echoed in her head.

Can we really pull this off? Or is the magic gone? Forever?

The smell of pine lingered on Brett as he set down the second box. The scent mixed with the faint wood smoke still clinging to the cabin air. "Almost done out there." He brushed at his sleeves that had bunched up on his forearms.

George nodded with crinkled eyes. "You all work well together. I can see it." He glanced at Alexis. The weight of his gaze pressed more than his words did. "Sarah used to say the same thing about us. We had our share of rough patches, but... Well." He sniffed rubbing a shirt sleeve over his eyes. "Life's a whole lot quieter now without her."

Alexis shifted on her feet not sure exactly what to say. She chewed on her lower lip. She couldn't escape the comparisons — the way George spoke about his late wife, the way Brett's presence beside her tugged at something unresolved. Divorce papers sat waiting for her signature, yet here she stood, working alongside the very man she'd vowed to leave behind.

But these two here tasks they completed, well they seemed to knit their lives together again, whether she wanted them to or not.

Brett brushed past her heading back outside. Alexis followed. The cold air bit at her skin. She pulled the edges of her jacket closer. She watched as he unloaded the final box of Bio block and neatly stack in the corner of George's porch.

As Brett finished up, the sun dipped lower in the sky. It cast a golden light over the snow-dusted trees making the scene almost picturesque. It conveyed a sense as if they belonged here together.

George stepped out onto the porch and leaned against the railing. He surveyed the job. "That'll keep me warm all winter. Couldn't have done it without you two." His voice cracked slightly on the last word. The weight of his loneliness palpable in the air. "Sarah would've been happy to see us all working together."

Alexis forced a smile nodding in acknowledgment. But inside, her mind raced. George's words stuck with her. His sentiment about partnership echoed in her thoughts.

Okay, we've worked well, so far. But can it last?

The scrunch of Brett stuffing his gloves into the pockets of his puffy vest caught Alexis' attention.

He wiped his hands on his jeans glancing at Alexis. "Guess we're done here."

The sound of her phone vibrating in her coat pocket broke the moment. She fished it out. The screen lit up with a message from Judge Henry. She frowned holding it up so Brett could see. "Tomorrow's deed." She read the text aloud. "Meet at the courthouse at 4 p.m. sharp. Tonight."

Brett raised an eyebrow. "What do you think it'll be this time?"

"I don't know." She stuffed the phone back into her pocket. Her chest tightened with an unfamiliar anxiety. The uncertainty of what lay ahead gnawed at her.

George chuckled behind them. The sound faded as they headed back to the truck. "Whatever it is, I reckon you all will handle it just fine. Always better when you've got someone by your side."

Alexis climbed into the truck. George's words gnawed at her thoughts long after they'd driven away from his cabin.

Always better when you've got someone by your side.

FROM: The Whiskey Tattler Editors
TO: Whiskey Tattler Subscribers
CC:
BCC:
Date: December 14th 11:32 am CST
Subject: Heating up with Love?

THE WHISKEY TATTLER

Branching Out with Bio Blocks
By Hazel and Harriet Montgomery
Deed Watch: Day Number Two
Task: Special Delivery

Well, darlings, after DAY 1 downtown decorating debacle — with Alexis and Brett nearly destroying Whiskey's Christmas tree — they've moved on to delivering a truckload of bio block, a fancy fertilizer chunk, don't ask us why, to the local Christmas tree farmer who lives just past the town limits. His wife passed last year, and rumor is he's talking to the trees more than to people — so our duo stepped in to offer a little green TLC.

Our editors have heard from reliable sources who stood off in the tree branches poking out, flapping like festive flags—only to find our farmer in his element knee-deep in sap, boots muddy enough to leave fingerprints in the Whiskey square. He's a sturdy chap—six foot something, wool cap pulled low, and all he needed was a friendly bio block to keep those firs growing strong.

Hazel:
"Delivering fertilizer to a widower — romantic or just practical?"
Harriet:
"If that tree grows faster than their marital flame, we're in trouble."
But we assure you: the vibe was more community service than Cupid's arrow. Still, there was something oddly sweet in the air — like evergreen and new beginnings.

Let's add some context: Christmas - tree farms are notorious for becoming holiday pilgrimage sites — complete with wagon rides, hot cocoa, and wall of memories, photo ops.

So, this Bio block delivery is more than just fertilizer. It's a gesture. A lifeline. Right?
And a reminder that life—and love—can sprout from even the most barren seasons.

Tomorrow's deed 3 involves ringing bells for charity (or maybe just ringing each other's bells), and we aren't sure whether we're looking at a donation drive—or a full-on duet with lots of mistletoe moments.

In summary:
Day 2 was light, whimsical, and wistful—fertilizer meets friendship on the farm. Stay tuned: day 3 might just ring in more than goodwill... and we'll be there with bell-rattling commentary.

Hazel and Harriet Montgomery,

Twins, Editors of the Whiskey Tattler, and Christmas Tree Huggers

Chapter 6

December 14th
The judge's chambers smelled of old wood and stale cigar smoke, the kind of room where decisions were carved out of silence. Brett sat on the edge of the stiff leather chair. The ticking of the wall clock filling the space between them and Alexis. The past few times they'd had to meet with the judge blurred together — a series of tense meetings and uncomfortable silences. And this wouldn't be any different.

Alexis shifted beside them, fingers tapping absently on the armrest. Brett didn't look over. He could already picture exactly what expression would be on Alexis' face. Instead, he stared straight ahead locking eyes with the framed picture of the judge shaking hands with some long-forgotten politician. That seemed easier than meeting Alexis' gaze.

The heavy door creaked open. The judge strolled in. His presence commanded as ever. His dark suit clung to his broad frame. The fabric stretching with his every move. Brett stiffened. He sat up straighter as the judge took his seat behind the large oak desk.

A thick folder landed with a soft thud in front of him. He flipped it open, brows furrowing slightly as he skimmed the pages inside. Brett's pulse quickened in the quiet room, each beat louder than the next. The sense of finality pressed down on his shoulders, making the air feel heavy.

The judge leaned back in his chair, steepling his fingers. His gaze shifted between Brett and Alexis before finally resting on Brett. The look pierced through the veneer of calm Brett tried to keep. It didn't matter that they had been here before — this time felt different. The tension between him and Alexis couldn't fix with apologies or promises. No, this thing between them resonated heavier, deeper.

Without preamble, the judge leaned forward. "This deed." The words, spoken slowly, carried a weight that filled the room. Brett clenched his hands in his lap, bracing for whatever came next.

Alexis shot a glance at Brett, but he didn't return it. Instead, he fixed his gaze on the judge willing the explanation to come faster. The judge, always one to relish in the pause, took his time. He tapped his finger on the desk, each tap grating against Brett's already frayed nerves.

Finally, the judge's gravelly voice broke the silence. "The town needs bells delivered."

Brett blinked.

Bells?

Of all the things, that seemed trivial. The confusion must have shown because the judge's lips curled into a faint smile, the kind that wasn't meant to reassure.

"Every year before Christmas, each household receives a bell. A tradition," he continued, his voice carrying the weight of something more than just bells. "This year, the two of you will be responsible for delivering them."

A bell delivery?

Brent exhaled sharply through his nose masking the rising frustration in his chest. He came here expecting something more — something that reflected the gravity of their situation. Delivering bells felt almost absurd. But the look in the judge's eyes suggested this wasn't up for negotiation.

Alexis shifted in the chair. Her posture stiffened as if the weight of the task pressed them down. Brett caught the briefest flicker of unease on Alexis' face before she quickly hid it behind the same mask she'd been wearing for weeks.

The judge's eyes lingered on both of them as if trying to gauge how well they'd handle this next hurdle. The silence that stretched between them held a question — one neither of them wanted to answer. Brett swallowed hard, unwilling to give the judge the satisfaction of seeing their discomfort.

"Start in the morning. Finish by sunset," the judge added, leaning back in his chair, signaling the end of the conversation.

The bell delivery wouldn't be just a simple task, more like a deadline. Another test.

Brett stood up first with hands stiff by his sides. The weight of the room, the judge's scrutiny, and Alexis's unspoken thoughts pressed down on him, making each movement feel heavier than the last. His throat tightened as he glanced over at Alexis. Something unsaid lingered between them. Something that hung like the unspoken truth neither could quite voice.

The judge's chair creaked as he rose. He moved toward the door. The scent of cigar smoke grew stronger as he neared them. His large hand rested briefly on Brett's shoulder, an unnecessary gesture that felt more like a warning than comfort. "Work together, It's not all about the bells."

Brett's jaw clenched.

Of course, it wasn't about the bells.

He followed Alexis out of the chambers. The echo of the door closing behind them rang in their ears. Outside, the air felt fresher, yet the pressure in Brett's chest remained. Alexis stood a few steps ahead with arms crossed staring down at the uneven sidewalk. Brett watched her for a moment trying to ignore the familiar ache in his chest — the same ache that had settled there when everything between them began unraveling.

This task, this absurd bell delivery, forced them to confront something neither of them had wanted to face, made possible only by the judge's decree. The road ahead had nothing to do with completing a task — no, it would prove whether or not they could work together one more time.

Brett took a deep breath. The smell of the faint scent of pine hung in the air. It had to be done, whether they liked it or not.

Alexis turned, meeting Brett's gaze with a look that held more questions than answers.

The sun began to lower over the horizon, casting long shadows across the street, marking the time they had left. He nodded, silently acknowledging the road ahead. No more hesitation with the task clear now, even though their future still hung in the air, they needed to move forward. Right?

FROM: The Whiskey Tattler Editors
TO: Whiskey Tattler Subscribers
CC:
Date: December 14th 9:01 am CST
Subject: Here comes the Judge!

THE WHISKEY TATTLER

The Judge and His Motives
By Hazel and Harriet Montgomery

Editorial Thoughts:
It's not often during this time of the year that we get to set down with Whiskey's finest judge since we discovered dipping sliced bananas with peanut butter and mayo, and not just any mayo, that special sandwich spread. Its miraculously quite tasty. But not to digress, we did. And the man who takes this great honor is none other than, Judge J. Henry.
Now most here think he's overstepped his judicial priorities, but frankly Whiskey isn't like most towns here in Texas.

Motives
The man hates divorce especially if you came to his courtroom and he presided over your marriage. Ahem... like a certain young couple who at the moment shall remain nameless.

Harriet's Side Note:
Remain nameless, don't think so. In fact, this couple is Alexis and Brett Stapleton. And they are about to ruin my friend's record as a judge. Shameless!

Let the Judge Explain:
"Well now, I've sat behind this bench long enough to know that love don't always need fixing — it just sometimes needs a dash of perspective to flood back in."

Chrissy Hartmann

"I've watched more broken hearts than dust storms out West — but when two folks clearly still hold on, my job's just to hand them a shovel and let them rediscover their own gold."

"In my court, I don't so much pass sentence as I light lanterns—helping people see what's been right in front of them all along."

The Plain Truth:

"I've seen couples come in lost as calves in a hailstorm — but if I can just help 'em stand and look at each other again — that's my kind of verdict."

"Out here, a judge's finest work ain't rulings—it's opening folks' eyes to love they still got. My method's simple: I stand aside, and let their hearts do the courting."

And there you have it folks. Straight from the horse's mouth. A man with a mission. And one darn good mission at that. SO, hold on to your tinsel cause this sleigh ride might get a little bumpy.

With bows and ribbon,

Hazel and Harriet Montgomery

Twins, Editors of the Whiskey Tattler, and Notable Tinsel Tossers

Chapter 7

December 15th
Deed Day number 3
The town square hummed with activity as Alexis glanced at Brett, who adjusted the box of bells. Her chest tightened briefly remembering they were supposed to be here together for this — before everything got complicated. Now, they had to deliver these bells as one of the judge's conditions for granting the divorce. Not the way she imagined spending their final days as a pair.

Brett nodded silently, signaling time to move.

Alexis gripped the handful of bells moving ahead.

The town came alive as the sun rose in the sky. Its energy surged around them with a handful of children laughing and darting around them.

Alexis wished the sight didn't tug at something deep inside. She stifled a sigh as she steered away from a group of vendors hoping to avoid unnecessary small talk.

The bells clinked with every movement. The sound a constant reminder of the task at hand. Memories flickered like old photographs — festivals they once attended before the silence and the distance between them grew louder. But now wasn't the time for sentimentality. The town needed its bells, and the judge needed proof they could work together, and it wouldn't mean a thing. No, nothing like strings attached, you know, those pesky love strings that attach themselves to ones heart without notice of it being too late.

Her brow furrowed with the uncertainty of the judge's motives.

Okay later. Worry about that later. Just deliver the bells.

They reached the church steps, where an elderly couple stood hand in hand. Alexis smiled at them, handing over a bell. Their wrinkled faces lit up, the woman's laughter ringing like the very bells they were giving out. She resisted the swell in her chest quickly shifting focus back to the box. After all, she wanted nothing that would get her caught up in an emotional rabbit hole. Alexis caught a glimpse of Brett's face as they walked. His expression softened, though it never stayed that way for long. She swallowed, brushing it off as the couple offered them grateful nods. In moments like this, the town became a mirror of what could have been — a community, a partnership, a life. She clenched the cluster of bells tighter and moved on.

Ahead, the sun cast a warm glow over the town's streets. Alexis glanced at the box. They still had quite a lot of bells to deliver. No time for daydreaming.

A stray dog trotted by sniffing the air curiously. It distracted Alexis for a brief moment from the mounting sense of unease. The day slipped away and so did the time together. Brett's quiet chuckle at the dog's antics broke the silence between them. Alexis's lips twitched into a faint smile, though the warmth didn't quite reach her chest.

As they approached the final homestead, an older man sat on his porch with eyes twinkling as he waited for them. Alexis handed him a bell. Their fingers brushed briefly. The man's gaze lingered with a knowing look that stirred something uncomfortable in her. She pulled away cocking her head as if she recognized the man.

Why did everyone in this town seem to understand things Alexis probably wouldn't want to admit to?

The box rattled lightly as they made their way back to the square. But the tension between Alexis and Brett grew heavier. Alexis stole a glance at Brett, who met it with a raised brow, silently asking the same question Alexis refused to answer.

The square filled with the soft glow of lanterns as they returned. The townsfolk gathered around in quiet celebration. The press of time pushed on her chest knowing the day's end meant more than just the close of this task.

They approached the judge's chambers. The heavy oak door stood between them and whatever came next. Alexis hesitated before stepping inside with Brett sidling up behind her. The cool wood of the door handle grounded her, but it didn't ease the tightness in her throat.

Inside, the judge barely looked up from his papers. His silence stretched on too long, and Alexis's pulse quickened in the quiet room. Her hands trembled slightly as they set the remaining bells down. Each one silently echoing the weight of unfinished business between them.

Alexis didn't speak at first, unsure where to start, or even if words would do anything now.

Brett stepped forward adding details here and there about their deliveries.

Alexis nodded along surprised at how easily Brett's voice filled the silence — how naturally they still moved through these things together. Like old habits refusing to die.

The judge finally looked back up. His gaze unreadable. Alexis' stomach twisted as he considered them, their shared work, their future. After a long, agonizing pause, the judge spoke. His voice calm and steady. He rocked back in his chair thumbs hooked into his belt, a sly grin pulling at the corner of his mouth. "Well, you all handled the bell delivery just fine, but now there's a new task on your plate." His eyes gleamed with that familiar mischief Alexis could never quite trust. "Hazel and Harriet Montgomery can't staff the Christmas dance ticket booth — they've got too much to handle with the dance prep. So, you two will take their place just outside Rupert's boutique of the best Whiskey has to offer in the Barleyshot Distillery's new place." His voice held that too-casual tone, the one that always made Alexis' stomach knot. Glancing over at Brett, she spotted the same flicker of confusion she felt.

"It's a small booth, cozy even," the judge added, amusement dancing in his eyes.

Cozy?

The word wrapped itself around Alexis like a noose, her suspicion tightening with each syllable. Crossing her arms, she studied the judge, but his grin only deepened, as if he held a secret — a secret they wouldn't discover until far too late.

No one spoke.

Alexis finally exhaled, though the tension didn't leave her body. It would take more than two charitable deeds to fix this. And now it looked as if they were on to the third.

FROM: The Whiskey Tattler Editors
TO: Whiskey Tattler Subscribers
CC:
Date: December 15th 5:02 pm CST
Subject: Holiday Eye Rolls

THE WHISKEY TATTLER

Ringing in Hope and an Eye Roll
By Hazel and Harriet Montgomery
Deed Watch: Day number Three
Task: Jingling the Judge's Bells

Deed three found the Stapletons gallivanting through town, delivering shiny Christmas bells to every household — "symbols of hope," they say. And honestly, what's more heartwarming than a bell at your doorstep?

According to holiday lore, bells once warded off evil spirits and now signify the arrival of good news and the birth of hope.

The pair hopped from porch to porch, setting jingle-tone intentions for the season. The townsfolk were delighted— some dabbed their eyes, others rang the bells spontaneously, and a few suspiciously checked if they owed a ticket for the honor.

Meanwhile, our resident judge T Henry — yes, that judge — has apparently handed out bells like candy for years. Hazel counted at least a dozen on record. Harriet wants you all to know, He's ringing more bells than a Salvation Army recruit on overtime." We wondered if judges could bankrupt an entire town just by overscheduling doorbell deliveries.

Still, we, the twins concede: the bells did bring a dose of goodwill. One grumpy hermit even admitted it "felt like getting a hug you didn't know you needed."
Forgive us if we didn't swoon—but it was sweet, in a crusted-over apple-pie kind of way.

What's Next? Tomorrow, our duo will be stationed at the Whiskey Ball's booth just outside of Ruperts new place, selling tickets to the Christmas Eve Ball. And rest assured, we'll personally ensure it's stocked with mistletoe—because it appears nothing's heating up yet, and God forbid our Whiskey have another holiday couple divorce. Who wants a breakup under the tinsel? Certainly not the folks here at the Whiskey Tattler.

Hazel and Harriet Montgomery

Twins, Editors of the Whiskey Tattler writing with bells on

Chrissy Hartmann

Chapter 8

December 16th

Brett sat behind the narrow counter of the booth. His knees bumped against hers as they both shifted to get comfortable. The space between them had little room for them to move. In fact, each time one shifted, He noticed it no matter how carefully they tried to avoid each other. The booth itself, drenched in Christmas decorations — tinsel, twinkling lights, and garlands — barely had room for both of them. And then, of course, a healthy sprig of mistletoe hung right over their heads — like the universe had some kind of twisted sense of humor.

He glanced at Alexis, who seemed entirely too focused on rearranging the ticket stubs in neat little piles and adjusting the Barleyshot cinnamon whiskey Christmas display. She avoided looking at him directly. With her jaw tight and flat smile, it signaled to Brett her discomfort. Hell, she probably wasn't thrilled about any of these "good deeds" the judge had assigned them. Neither of them had expected their divorce proceedings to come with Christmas chores.

A burst of WARM air from the entrance TO Rupert's boutique rushed toward the ticket boot. Brett's head snapped up to find his soon to be ex-wife's mood change. Her eyes suddenly lit up as an elderly woman approached bundled in a red scarf and carrying a basket full of oranges. Alexis greeted her with a warm smile, that same charm she'd always had, and launched into the ticket sales pitch before the woman had even fully reached the counter. "Whiskey's Christmas Eve Ball is going to be something special this year., you wouldn't want to miss it?"

The woman grinned back as she fished for her wallet in her purse.

Without missing a beat, Alexis continued. "That's a beautiful scarf. Did you make it?"

The woman laughed. "Oh goodness no. I could never be so talented."

Alexis held up two tickets. "Well, the colors are wonderful with your complexion."

The woman blushed. "Oh, thank you."

Brett nodded. "She's right."

And within the moment, the woman handed over cash for the tickets. "Thank you. You're so sweet."

Alexis slid the bills over to Brett who picked them up and placed them in the cash box. "We hope you have a lovely time at the dance."

The woman left beaming, clutching her tickets like they were a golden invitation to some grand event. Pride swelled in Brett's chest.

She's still got it.

The effortless charm she paid on someone could make anyone feel like they were the only person in the room. An effortless attention that he couldn't remember how she'd ever drawn him in with it.

His lips curled to one side.

And yes, it had been one of the many reasons, he'd fallen so hard, so fast.

More customers trickled by the booth. Each time, Alexis worked her magic. She sold the tickets with a combination of genuine warmth and just the right amount of persuasion. For most of the time, Brett watched. A few times, he pretended to help.

Okay, man. Get it together. We're divorcing.

He raked a hand threw his hair. He blew out his breath. His heart thumped against his chest in an S.O.S. pattern.

Don't go there.

Her elbow brushed against him as she handed a flyer to an older man. The touch sent a jolt through him. It caught him off guard. His eyes drifted to the mistletoe above them. It hung like a silent reminder of how much had changed — and how much hadn't.

The lack of space only stirred things he hadn't wanted to deal with. He mentally swept those thoughts away with each flyer he handed out as a distraction.

The crowd finally thinned leaving the booth quiet. Alexis propped herself against the booth and took a deep breath. Her eyes closed for a moment. Then exhaling, she smiled with her eyes studying the incoming shoppers.

Brett in turn did the same, but with a smirk on his face. He studied Alexis instead.

Her fingers tapped absently on the table.

With the moment of silence drawing longer between them, Brett pointed to the depleted stack of tickets. "You're great at this."

Alexis' lips twitched into a faint smile, but she didn't respond. Instead, she leaned forward. Her eyes followed a family of four walking by as they came in through the front doors. The parents wrangled two excited kids. Her expression softened, but just for a second. Then she straightened with a guarded look returning.

The smell of pine trailed in the families wake as the front doors slowly closed. A Christmas tree lot stood outside the doors just near the parking lot. Brett inhaled deeply. The uptick of a smile formed. But the calmness that enveloped him with the scent of the outdoors dissipated when he shifted to find Alexis staring up at the mistletoe.

Her lips pressed into a tight line.

His stomach flipped. The moment stretched. The weight of the mistletoe lingered above them. The sprig hung over them as if daring them to do something. He shifted slightly. His elbow brushed hers again.

Her breath caught —

And in that second, their eyes locked.

Alexis leaned in.

His heart pounded against his chest. He didn't move, didn't dare ruin the moment. The magnetic pull between them stronger than anything they'd managed to fight off for the last few days if not months.

Heat rose between them despite the festive chill of the store. But just as their lips almost met, a throat cleared behind them.

Brett jerked back, straightening as Judge Henry's unmistakable voice cut through the awkward silence.

"Well, now," His tone thick with amusement. "It's good to see you two working so closely. Almost got yourselves caught under the mistletoe, eh?"

Brett ran a hand through his hair chuckling under his breath. The absurdity of the situation wasn't lost on him, especially considering how they'd almost kissed while on the verge of divorce. But he didn't laugh because of the almost kiss, no not at all. The chuckles he tried to suppress only came from the frustration he spotted on Alexis' face — her RICH BROWN eyes slamming shut a low growl slipping past her lips.

He cocked his head. His eyes danced. Hmm? What if...

Judge Henry strode over to them. His boots clacked against the tile floor. "Alright, you two. Time for your next assignment." He held out a slip of paper, one eyebrow arched in that way only he could manage. "Christmas trees and food deliveries for the shut-ins. You start tomorrow morning."

Alexis took the paper. Her jaw clenched, clearly not thrilled about the prospect of more time spent together. Brett, on the other hand, just grinned. Delivering Christmas trees and groceries wouldn't be so bad, and honestly, it gave him an excuse to keep figuring out what she had going on in that pretty head of hers.

The judge tipped his hat, walking off with a casual wave. The moment he disappeared, Brett leaned against the counter again, a lazy smile tugging at his lips. "Almost got caught there."

Alexis shot him a glare, folding the slip of paper into her pocket. She said nothing, her eyes narrowing as if daring him to make another joke about it. But he couldn't resist. "Mistletoe has a funny way of working, doesn't it?" His smile widened, a glint of mischief in his eyes. "Not sure if you're madder that we almost kissed...or that we didn't."

Alexis' cheeks flushed, her mouth opening as if to respond, but no words came out. Instead, she huffed, pushing away from the counter as if the conversation had exhausted her.

Brett chuckled softly to himself. He watched her retreat.

Hmm? Despite the awkward tension between us, she hadn't entirely hated the almost-kiss.

Tomorrow's deed awaited them, but tonight, as Brett gathered up the last of the ticket stubs. Ideas rolled in his thought like a tumbleweed over the pasture — gently bouncing from one thought to another, never seeming to find a final resting place.

And what might come next intrigued him more than he wanted to admit.

He humphed.

Mistletoe or not, There's still something between us. And for the first time in a long while, he found himself wondering where this Christmas season would lead.

FROM: The Whiskey Tattler Editors
TO: Whiskey Tattler Subscribers
CC:
BCC:
Date: December 16th 8:04 pm CST
Subject: Mistletoe Kisses... Or Not?

THE WHISKEY TATTLER

Keeping an eye out from the dairy aisle.
By Hazel and Harriet Montgomery
Deed Watch: Day Number Four
Task: That's the Ticket!

As seasoned booth-survivors ourselves, ask us about the 1978 Great Cabbage Caper, we know every inch counts. You shift, they shift — space vanishes faster than mince pies at midnight—until the air itself hints at "something more."

Enter the mistletoe question:
Have. They. Kissed. Yet?
Hazel's hunch:

Absolutely, albeit quickly—like swiping the last Christmas ham.

Me, I counter her thought,

No way — they've been too busy chatting up the customers on the details of the Christmas Ball and how many bottles of cinnamon whiskey will be available that night.

But here's the twist:

the distillery owner, yes, that rascal known for theatrics, Jack Barleyshot himself has whipped up a cinnamon whiskey — think corn whiskey, cinnamon-leaf oil, and cane sugar — and is dangling a bottle at each couple who buys a ticket.

Well, to be honest, Jack's only dangling it metaphorically. The man's too busy to man the booth. But he did provide a beautiful display.
One can only imagine the scent of cinnamon cutting through that shared breath zone. Suddenly the booth's not nearly big enough for two.

Naturally, Hazel noted that "close proximity + cinnamon whiskey = the fastest way to smooches since gas-station petrol pumps." And I of course ever the skeptic, quipped, "Or at least a very hearty sniff-and-smile." Either way, we insist that mistletoe — real or imagined — was working overtime in that confined space.

EDITORS NOTE:
Jack reminds us that no full cinnamon whiskey bottles were on hand for today's deed. Just one dandy of a display. And no tickets will be sold to minors. Sales will continue until the 23rd. So, shine up them boots and you ladies warm up your dancing shoes, cause we want those spurs jingling!

So, dear readers, keep your eyes peeled (and your noses unlocked). Between the ticket-selling tango, spicy whiskey aroma, and booth-level intimacy, we're betting there was a moment under that mistletoe— whether poetic or panic driven.

Tune in tomorrow for Deed 5, when our couple tackles task #5 — The Polar Opposites Test, involving delivering much needed items for the shut-ins of Whiskey.
Will the heart deliver or will the chill in the air put a freeze on romance? We'll be there, thermos and marshmallows in hand.

Harriet and Hazel Montgomery,

Twins, Editors of the Whiskey Tattler, and the official Barleyshot Distillery cinnamon connoisseurs

Chapter 9

December 17th

Alexis wiped her hands on her jeans watching as Mrs. Rumsted shuffled back into her small living room. Her smile lingered from their visit. The door creaked shut, the sound soft but final, as if it marked the end of something larger than just the delivery.

Her old high school teacher had hugged her so tightly. The scent of lavender clinging to her cardigan, murmuring how wonderful to see them together again.

Together?

The word hung in the air like mist, hard to grasp, yet impossible to ignore.

Beside her, Brett leaned against the truck, arms crossed, a playful smirk tugging at his lips. He glanced sideways at her. The glint in his eyes unmistakable. "Well," he drawled, the corner of his mouth lifting higher, "that's it. The last tree delivered. Looks like we're done."

Alexis tensed, her throat tightening as she stared at him.

Done?

Did he mean the deliveries, or something more?

The word pierced through her, sinking deeper than she wanted to admit. Silence pressed down on her, the unspoken words between them almost too heavy to bear.

Brett uncrossed his arms, taking a step toward her, the gravel and snow crunching under his boots. Without warning, he reached out, his fingers brushing a stray lock of hair from her face, tucking it behind her ear. His hand lingered for a moment, and then he leaned in, his lips grazing her temple in the gentlest of kisses. A warmth spread through her chest, catching her off guard, his familiar scent of pine and sandelwood stirring up memories she'd pushed down for far too long.

The sound of the sugar plumb fairies tune coming from her pocket jolted her from his touch.

Her hands dug into her coat pocket. She fumbled with her phone, grateful for the distraction when it sang out in her pocket. She glanced at the screen, a message from the judge lighting up the display.

Next deed tomorrow: Whiskey Salvation Shelter, 9 A.m. for cookie baking.

Alexis pressed her lips together, holding back a laugh.

Of course, it had to be cookies.

She slipped the phone back into her pocket and turned to Brett, raising an eyebrow. "Looks like tomorrow's deed is right up my alley. Cookie baking at the Whiskey Salvation Shelter."

"You still can't cook to save your life," he teased, his voice low, "but those Christmas cookies of yours..." He trailed off, his smile widening as if they shared a secret no one else could understand.

Alexis blinked, her heart skipping a beat. The tenderness in his words surprised her, disarmed her. She swallowed hard, trying to compose herself.

Baking cookies? After everything, that's what he remembered?

Brett chuckled, his eyes twinkling as he leaned back against the truck again. "Well, those there at the shelter sure are lucky. And won't they be in for a treat."

Alexis forced a playful smirk, trying to match his easy tone, but something deeper churned beneath her façade. The way he remembered her cookies after all these years — the way he still teased her about them — warmed a part of her she thought had long cooled. His words, his touch, even his teasing kiss — all of it tugged at strings she hadn't realized were still attached. But she couldn't let him see that, not now. Not after everything.

He pushed off the truck, stretching his arms above his head, his movements slow and relaxed, as if he hadn't a care in the world. "Ready to go?"

Alexis bit on her bottom lip as she stuck her phone back into her coat.

He laughed, climbing into the driver's seat, leaving her standing there, staring after him. The sound of the truck door closing snapped her out of her daze. She shook her head, walking around to the passenger side and slid in. His easy smile stayed with her, long after they drove away from Mrs. Rumstead's house, but so did the quiet weight of his words. Inside, questions swirled, unspoken but persistent.

Could he really still care, after everything? Or had the judge's silly deeds just brought us together for a fleeting moment, a holiday illusion of what once had been?

As they drove down the road, Alexis stared out the window watching the lights of Whiskey twinkle as they passed by. The town seemed ready for Christmas, but she wasn't so sure about her own heart.

The judge's text might have mentioned cookies, but her thoughts had drifted far from flour and sugar. Brett had kissed her temple, a sweet, simple gesture, and it lingered on her skin, warming her long after the contact ended. He still remembered her cookies. He still teased her. And maybe, just maybe, he still cared.

Tomorrow would come soon enough, and with it, another deed. But tonight, as the truck's tires hummed against the road and Brett's quiet presence filled the space beside her, Alexis couldn't help but wonder if the judge had a bigger plan in mind. After all, twelve deeds could bring more than just Christmas cheer.

Couldn't it?

The truck slowed pulling alongside the curb just outside a quaint bed and breakfast, the Wildflower Bunkhouse. The engine idled as Alexis pulled herself from her thoughts. Snow drifted down in large fluffy snowflakes.

"Alexis?"

She glanced at the inn and then to Brett. Her mouth opened slightly as if she wanted to say something, but nothing fell past her lips. Her mind raced with questions on how it had all gone wrong and why neither of them did anything of real value to salvage their marriage.

But then Brett threw the truck into park. He leaned closer to her and with only a whisper away his warm breath caressed her skin. Her insides tingled. "I had fun today."

Alexis' eyes widened. "You did?"

He nodded. "Do you need a ride tomorrow?"

Not sure how to process that comment, Alexis slowly shook her head. "No, it's only a few blocks away and I've not heard of any snowstorms blowing in any time soon."

The faintest hint of disappointment crossed Bret's face, but melted away like the snowflakes hitting the windshield. He then glanced at her with a grin. "Guess I'll meet you at the shelter tomorrow, Cookie Queen."

Alexis rolled her eyes as she pulled on the door handle, but the corners of her mouth twitched upward in spite of herself. "Don't forget your apron."

FROM: The Whiskey Tattler Editors
TO: Whiskey Tattler Subscribers
CC:
BCC:
Date: December 17ᵗʰ 5:05 pm CST
Subject: Door Dash to Love?

THE WHISKEY TATTLER

"Groceries & Glee
By Hazel Montgomery
Deed Watch: Day Number Five
Task: A Yuletide Haul

Today had us, the duo donning mittens and marshmallow-smiles as Alexis and Brett delivered grocery packs and Christmas trees to the town's shut-ins. Think of it as Meals on Wheels with a festive twist—and a side of spicy snark courtesy of yours truly.

The Grand Toll:
• 22 homes were visited (plus one curl-up recliner that splintered under the weight—oops).
• 18 shut-ins gratefully accepted the groceries, offering thank-you waves that nearly knocked Brett, the driver off the porch.
• 4 suspicious souls eyed the couple like they were door-to-door carolers with ulterior motives — "Are they here for the groceries or the gossip?" one muttered.

Treats Included:
• Homemade shortbread cookies (a recipe older than Hariet (HO! HO! HO!), but still tacky enough to attract attention).
• Mini cinnamon-sugar pumpkin breads—sweet enough to make even a curmudgeon murmur, "Well, that's nice."
• And my favorite, a packet of hot cocoa mix, because nothing says "you're not forgotten" like a cup of warmth.

Hazel's tongue-in-cheek take?
"You could cut the gratitude with a butter knife — just don't ask if I meant the cookies or the gossip."

Sweet gestures, brisk visits, and a twinkle of holiday hope—all wrapped in peppermint-striped bags.

Chrissy Hartmann

Stay tuned for tomorrow's deed. We hear its hot and sweet!

Hazel Montgomery,

Co-Editor of the Whiskey Tattler and your ever-curious and slightly mischievous twin

Chapter 10

December 18th

Deed Day Number 6 Brett stood in front of the counter at the Whiskey Salvation Shelter, staring at the assortment of baking supplies laid out like some sort of twisted challenge. Flour, sugar, butter, eggs. Bowls of brightly colored frosting lined the table, and in the corner, a mixer whirred like a machine waiting to sabotage his entire day. Christmas cookie duty. Of all the things the judge could've assigned them to do, making cookies ranked somewhere between torture and unnecessary suffering in his book. And worst of all, it didn't look like they'd be making her candy cane cookies. No candy canes. Lots of frosting and sprinkles though .

Brett blew out his breath.

He glanced over at Alexis, who already rolled up her sleeves and eyed the cookie cutters like a pro. Sure, she might be a party planner in the city, but he'd eaten her Christmas cookies before, but create them with her, well he'd never done it or at least not that he could remember. And ultimately, when it came down to it, he hated pretending like he enjoyed this. But eating them, well that there he had no problem with. But there were a million other things he could be doing — like working on that project back at his house. Alexis' voice pulled him out of his thoughts.

"What's that look for?" She smirked. Flour dusted her hands as she pressed a round cookie cutter into the dough.

Brett shrugged. "This just isn't my kind of thing."

Alexis tilted her head, eyebrows raised. "You'd rather be in your workshop, wouldn't you?"

"Of course." He tossed a glance toward the door as if contemplating escape. "Got a project I'm working on. Something I need to finish before Christmas."

"What kind of project? Is it for someone special?" She leaned in fishing for details, eyes gleaming like she might have an idea already.

"Nope." Brett straightened up, grabbing a nearby cookie cutter and attempting to contribute without making a total mess. "Can't talk about it until after Christmas."

Alexis narrowed her eyes. Her smile faltered for just a bit. She pressed harder. "Why not? Is it top secret? Maybe something for a lady friend?"

His grip on the cookie cutter tightened. Brett turned back to the dough avoiding her gaze. "Not talking about it."

That did it. Alexis' mouth thinned, and she set down the rolling pin with more force than necessary.

Brett could practically see the wheels turning in her head, wondering if anyone else could.

Truth be told, the project didn't have anything to do with another woman, but saying so might open up a whole new can of worms he wasn't ready to deal with.

After a minute of silence, Alexis huffed and reached for the frosting. She dipped a spatula into the bowl. She slathered a thick layer onto a cookie. But now, her movements were quick and sharp. Irritation lingered in the air between them, thicker than the smell of vanilla extract.

Brett raised an eyebrow and watched as she attacked another cookie with the frosting like it had personally offended her. He picked up his own frosting knife, slow and deliberate, eyeing the perfectly neat lines she made on her cookie. He smirked to himself and reached over, dragging his finger through the middle of her frosted cookie leaving a long messy wake of green frosting.

Alexis gasped. Her eyes blew open in disbelief. She growled under her breath. And without a word, she grabbed a handful of sprinkles and flung them at him. Most of them landed squarely in his hair. Brett grinned, not missing a beat, and flicked a dollop of red frosting toward her, hitting her apron.

"Really?" She stepped back and stared at the frosting as it slid down her apron. She dipped her hand into another bowl, this time loaded with blue icing, and swiped it across his forearm, leaving a trail of sticky sweetness in her wake.

Brett laughed and retaliated with a swipe of frosting to her cheek.

The food fight escalated quickly. Soon, they were both covered in an array of colors, frosting splattered across the countertops, sprinkles scattered on the floor like confetti. Brett leaned in, ready for his next attack when his hand brushed her face. The touch lingered. The softness sank into his fingertips. His heart skipped a beat.

Alexis paused. Her smile faded as she met his eyes. The room stilled. The chaos around them faded into the background. Her breath hitched. Brett couldn't move, couldn't break away from the pull between them. His hand lingered near her face, thumb brushing her bottom lip. His heart pounded against his chest.

The temperature in the room rose.

They stood close now, real close. Frosting forgotten. Only inches between them now. His gaze dropped to her lips. His hovered dangerously close to hers. Just one step forward. Just one lean in. And —

A loud cough interrupted them. Brett snapped out of the moment.

Harriet and Hazel, stood at the door, grinning like they'd walked in on the punchline of a joke they weren't supposed to witness.

Hazel crossed her arms. "Well, isn't this cozy." Her eyes twinkled with amusement as she surveyed the mess. "Looks like we missed out on some kind of frosting war."

Harriet chuckled beside her shaking her head. "Judge sent us to check in on you two, but looks like you all are having plenty of fun."

Brett cleared his throat, backing away from Alexis. He attempted to wipe the frosting off his hands with a dishtowel. "Just getting things...sorted."

Alexis wiped at her face with the back of her hand as if nothing had happened. "What brings you two here, exactly?"

Harriet exchanged a glance with Hazel before pulling a folded piece of paper from her pocket. "Judge lent you out to us for tomorrow's Christmas tea at the senior center. Antiquers' Christmas tea. You'll be serving tea and handing out these cookies, so I hope you all haven't destroyed half of them."

Hazel added, "Oh, and you've gotta make about five more batches. Seniors are hungry around the holidays, you know."

Brett groaned inwardly.

Cookies. More cookies. At this rate, we'll be swimming in sugar and sprinkles by the end of the week.

He watched Alexis. He half-expected her to explode at the news. Nope. No explosions. But instead, she looked...surprised, maybe even amused. Typical of the judge to throw them into one situation after another.

She glanced at Brett. A smirk tugged at the corners of her lips. "Tea party, huh? Guess you better work on your cookie decorating skills."

Hazel clapped Brett on the shoulder. "Good luck, cowboy. You're gonna need it."

As the two women left, Brett stood there staring at the mess they'd made, both of cookies and their almost-kiss. The frosting still clung to his shirt, but for once, he wasn't sure he cared.

Whoa! What almost happened here? Does she really still have a hold on me? Even after everything?

Alexis interrupted his thoughts, soft but laced with mischief. "You're terrible at keeping secrets, you know that, right?"

Brett turned, his heart still thumping a little faster than it should. "What makes you say that?"

She rolled her eyes and grabbed a clean towel. Then with the flick of her wrist she tossed it to him. "You're awful at avoiding questions. I'll get the truth out of you eventually."

Grinning, Brett wiped the frosting from his arms watching her out of the corner of his eye. Tomorrow would bring more cookies, more awkward proximity, and maybe — just maybe — another chance for something to shift between them.

FROM: The Whiskey Tattler Editors
TO: Whiskey Tattler Subscribers
CC:
Date: December 18th 12:04 pm CST
Subject: Frosting... Sprinkles... Oh my!

THE WHISKEY TATTLER

Cookies & Curiosities
By Hazel and Harriet Montgomery
Deed Watch: Day Number Six
Task: Naughty or nice, you decide!

This day whisked our couple into the prim, polished world of the Antiquers' Christmas Tea, where today's task was frosting and adorning Christmas cookies.

They set to work with the usual suspects, cut-out frosted Christmas cookies — trees, stars, bells — for painting with icing dye.

Believe it or not, after the scene we walked in on, never thought to see such beautifully revered—Victorian meets village-chic as the cookies dusted silver trays and took care to keep the icing smooth and lovely.

Convivial commentary from Harriet:

Hogwash! They were piping and slathering with sprinkles flying like confetti while we stood and watched from the door. One cookie looked so lopsided I thought it might moonlight as a frisbee. Never imagined they could get them looking this delicious. Guess this is the season for miracles.

Mission Report:

• Thirty trays decorated (10 per type).
• We snapped several photos of the frosted creations for our files.
• Brett and Alexis even charmed these two particularly snooty Antiquers with whispers about nostalgic cookie cutters from childhood.

It was a scene simmered in tradition, but our couple handled it with a touch of grace. And we do mean a touch — not too much elbowing, not too many icing drips on the floor, or sprinkles in the hair. Bravo!

Chrissy Hartmann

Sneak Peek:
For tomorrow's deed number 7, they'll don Mr. & Mrs. Santa Claus outfits — yes, full red suits, hats, and a faux beard — to serve the Antiquers for their many contributions over the years at the Whiskey Christmas Tea party... We hope!

Yours in sugar and sass,

Hazel and Harriet Montgomery,

Twins, Editors of the Whiskey Tattler, and Christmas Cookie Connoisseurs

Chapter 11

December 19th

Deed Day Number 7Alexis balanced a tray of Christmas cookies in one hand while attempting to pour tea with the other. She plastered a forced smile across her face as Hazel and Harriet fluttered around Brett like moths to a flame. Both women, dressed in their finest holiday sweaters and red jumpers, practically swooned every time he so much as shifted his weight in his red pants and black boots. And lets not forget to mention the spurs. In fact, most of the women attending won't ever either.

"Mr. February," Hazel declared, tapping her finger against her lips. "Wouldn't he just be perfect, Harriet? Our Whiskey Valentine!"

Harriet nodded like a jackrabbit hopping. "Oh, yes! Can't you just see him in a black cowboy hat, holding a bouquet of roses? All the ladies would swoon!"

Alexis choked on a laugh as she set the teapot down before she spilled it. She rolled her eyes. "Roses and Brett? He's more likely to show up with a bag of nails than a bouquet."

Brett glanced in her direction with lips twitching.

Alexis caught the glance even if the man tried to hide his annoyance by arranging the cups of tea in front of the seniors, but the flush that crept up his neck suggested otherwise as it almost matched the color of his Santa Jacket.

Hazel and Harriet continued their campaign oblivious to anyone around them. "We've already got Mr. January locked down ." Hazel counted on her fingers. "But Mr. February — oh, he's got to be our cowboy here." She fluttered her eyelashes at him like a twenty-year-old, not a seventy something.

Alexis leaned in closer to Brett. "Looks like you've got a modeling career ahead of you. I can just see the headlines: 'From carpenter Rancher to Runway'."

Brett scowled — sort of. "They're not serious, are they?"

Alexis swirled her red velvet skirt while turning with an empty platter. She covered her mouth trying not to laugh. "Oh, they're dead serious. If you thought the Santa suit bad, then wait until February. You're about to be the face of Whiskey's finest Valentine. And nice touch with those spurs."

He groaned under his breath shaking his head. He leaned over one of the Antiquers and poured a cup of tea. "You think this is funny, don't you?"

Alexis raised an eyebrow as she approached the table with a fresh tray of cookies and offered one to a member of the Antiquers. "Hilarious."

The truth? Alexis loved watching Brett squirm under the attention of the Antiquer ladies, which brought more joy than it probably should. After all, it wasn't every day someone else had to deal with that level of small-town charm, but then again, Brett always did attract attention without even trying. Something about the quiet confidence he carried, wrapped in that unbothered, rugged look.

A quick glance in his direction confirmed her thoughts. His red suit jacket clung to broad shoulders. He'd rolled up his sleeves giving just enough to reveal tanned forearms, showing off the taught muscles he'd developed over the years working on their small ranch. And his thick dark chocolate hair, well any sane woman would love to run her fingers through it, even the crazy ones too.

Holy smokes, what am I thinking. Stop that. Only a few more days and then you'll be divorced. Now concentrate. Tea. Cookies. Nothing else.

But her eyes didn't get the message from her brain. Nope, they strayed back to where he stood. And in her defense, not hard to do when the cowboy wore the only pair of spurs that afternoon. Just listen for the jingle jangle. And no not talking about Santa either.

Argh!

Alexis shook the thought away.

Good deeds — nothing more.

She grabbed another platter of cookies.

Christmas cookies and tea. Focus, Alexis.

The event passed in a blur of laughter and harmless flirtation from the seniors. The platters of cookies disappeared at an impressive rate, and the tea kept flowing as the room buzzed with festive cheer.

With her feet aching from the knee-high boots she wore with her costume all afternoon, her need to take the leather boots with their three-inch heels off overshot any need for cleanup. And anyway, with most of the guests gone, no one would care if she took off the ankle breakers. So, scanning the room, she found a small alcove she could use. Not mentioning what she wanted to do, she slipped into the alcove and sat on the bench seat she found. She sighed once she sat down. "Ah yeah." She closed her eyes and breathed. As the sensation flowed back into her toes, she lifted one boot, but before she could do anything, the jingle jangle of spurs broke the silence. Then large hands wrapped around the ankle of her lifted foot. Her eyes shot open. Brett.

"Uh, high. Just taking a quick break."

Brett smiled. "Your feet hurt, don't they?"

She shook her head biting on her bottom lip.

He chuckled. "Liar. I know you. You don't wear shoes over an inch tall."

"Brett, please." She pulled back her leg. The hem of her skirt slid back. She clutched at the hem.

The corner of his lips rose a tick on one side. He ran his hands up and down the polished black leather. His fingers stopped at the zipper tab. "Can I?"

She shook her head. Her heart thudded against her chest. Her lips were dry as the words passed over them. "Brett, no. This isn't a good idea."

His other hand ran down the length of her leg massaging it as it reached her ankle. "You sure, Darling? You might feel better."

Oh yeah, I'd feel better. But…"

The warmth of his hands sank into the leather heating her up on the inside. Her eyes closed. The curls constrained by the candy cane scarf she wore fell backwards as she sank into the massage. His hands on her made her muscles scream in delight. Her heart kept whispering —more, more, need more.

Bret leaned into her ear with the slightest brush of his whiskers grazing her cheek. The grainy touch reminded her of days long past. A smile curled on her lips, she giggled.

"You still don't want me to remove your boot?"

She gave a little shake of her head.

His fingers massaged deeper. "Sure? Last chance."

"Ahem." A crackled voice came from the doorway.

"Harriet, I found them." Hazel chuckled. " Looks as if Mrs. Claus is having trouble with her boots."

Alexis' eyes shot open. She scooched back on the bench pulling Brett with her. She peeked over his shoulder. Her face immediately colored to match the Santa jacket. "Uh, hello ladies."

Harriet now behind Hazel pushed on her sister to get a better view. "Well land sakes. You two done horsing around? We've got to finish cleaning up here."

Brett gave her ankle one last squeeze as he lowered it to the ground. He chuckled shaking his head. "Leave it to them."

Alexis' brows rose.

Them?

She sighed. "Yes, all finished here. Just had something in my boot and Brett wanted to make sure I got it out." Her voice lifted in a fake cheery note. "All good, promise."

Brett turned. "Ladies, my work here is done, now if you'll excuse me, I think there's some cookies that need tending to."

Both Antiquers gave him the eagle eye as he passed by them. "Make sure to box those cookies up, I think you've had enough sugar for the day."

Brett through up a thumb.

"You need a minute to collect yourself?" Hazel pushed on her glasses. "Harriet and I will be collecting the linens if you need any more help."

Harriet leaned into her sister. "I don't think she needs our help."

Hazel shook her head with a tisk, tisk.

And on those words, Alexis jumped up with only the slightest pinch to her toes as she dashed out of the alcove. "No, ma'am, I got this." But just as Alexis began cleaning up the last of the mess, she noticed something that stopped her mid-swipe.

Brett stood near the door, a light smile on his face as he talked to someone. Someone she didn't recognize. And this someone, a woman. She had blonde hair, styled perfectly, not a strand out of place, and wore a bright green coat that screamed Christmas chic. The two chatted for a moment and then... Brett smiled. One of those warm, easy smiles that usually took some effort and a lot of patience to pull from him.

A twinge of tightness pulled at Alexis' insides — deeply. The grip she held on the tray faltered. Her breathing stopped.

The woman leaned in closer to Brett, whispered something, and then, without so much as a glance back toward Alexis, he followed the mystery woman out the door.

The tray clattered against the counter drawing the attention of one of the other volunteers. "You alright, honey?"

Alexis forced a smile. "Yeah, just...dropped something."

The curiosity that simmered beneath her skin turned to a slow burn.

Who's that? A date?

And why hadn't he mentioned anything about dating? The divorce isn't even finalized yet. And what was that whole thing back there with my boots?

For days, they'd been stuck in this holiday deed circus together, thrown into awkward situations, decorating, baking cookies, and now this. And in all that time, he hadn't so much as hinted that he might be seeing someone.

Alexis stormed back to the cookie table tossing the last of the napkins into the trash with more force than necessary. What did it matter, anyway? They were on the verge of ending things. Still, something about the whole situation left a bitter taste in her mouth.

Judge Henry arrived just as she scrubbed the last stubborn spot off the counter. His boots clomped against the floor. Alexis barely managed to avoid rolling her eyes at his impeccable timing.

"Heard everything went quite well today. Only cookie crumbles and tea leaves left." He adjusted his hat with a satisfied grin. "Got another good deed for you tomorrow."

Alexis grabbed a towel and wiped her hands.

"Gift wrapping at the Whiskey Salvation Shelter. For the kids. Big turnout this year, so get some good sleep — you'll need it."

She let out a slow breath, dropping the towel onto the counter. "Fine. Wrapping presents. Got it."

The judge tipped his hat and exited the room, leaving her alone to stew in her own thoughts. Wrapping presents. At least that would be something she could focus on — something to keep her mind off the scene she'd just witnessed. But as she stood there, in the now-empty room, her mind kept wandering back to Brett.

Who's the woman? Why hasn't he said anything about her?

The frustration built with each unanswered question. Alexis found herself glaring at the door as if it held all the answers. Maybe the divorce couldn't come fast enough. Maybe the tiredness of the whole situation had finally set in. Maybe...maybe she still cared more than she wanted to admit.

She twisted her hair into a messy bun and grabbed her purse and marched toward the door. There'd be no peace of mind tonight, not with those questions gnawing at her. As she flicked off the light and locked the door behind her, one question lingered though. Had Brett decided to move on without her?

FROM: The Whiskey Tattler Editors
TO: Whiskey Tattler Subscribers
CC:
Date: December 19th 4:21 pm CST
Subject: Tea and Cookies with Santa

The Whiskey Tattler

Spreading Christmas cheer — whether wanted or not.
By Hazel and Harriet Montgomery
Deed Watch: Day number Eight
TASK: Antiquers Christmas tea party

Someone please tell us who let Brett, "stoic" Stapleton wear velvet and spurs.

Because there he stood — red suit, fake beard, and that deer-in-headlights look — next to Alexis whose Mrs. Claus costume was cuter than any woman has a right to look when she's supposed to be divorced.

There were ho-ho-ho's, dropped selfie bombings, a malfunctioning music speaker (someone tell Stan from IT to stop "fixing" things with duct tape), and one intense round pouring tea where Alexis might have threatened a retiree over a disputed second plate of cookies.

Hazel's Breakdown:
Number of times Brett forgot he was Santa: 4
Number of times he said "Darlin'" and made the women over seventy swoon: Too many to count.
Alexis' fake laugh-to-real laugh ratio: 3:2 by our estimate
Then there was the moment. Y'all know the one.
Brett tried to help her out of her Santa boots — (cue the choir) — and we swear he looked at her like she was the last peppermint in the tin.
Rumors have it when Mildred from the bakery heard about it, she fainted. Again.

Harriet's Note:
They didn't kiss. Yet.

Hazel's Retort:
Give it time. The beard's coming off eventually.

Chrissy Hartmann

Stay tuned for deed number 8 community wrapping presents at the Whiskey Salvation Shelter. Nothing says love like ribbon wrapped around your neck.

Hazel and Harriet Montgomery,

Twins, Editors of the Whiskey Tattler, and champion Tea Sippers of Texas

December 20th

Deed Day Number 8Brett grabbed another gift box from the pile, the thin red tartan paper crinkling in his hands as he tried to fold the edges. Neatness never came naturally to him, but Alexis? She wrapped presents like she'd spent years doing it professionally. Every corner precise, every bow tied exactly right. He stared at his own sad attempt, the tape crooked, the red tartan paper sagging. She hadn't said a word about it, but her silence spoke volumes.

The shelter buzzed with Christmas energy, boxes everywhere, the faint hum of a caroling playlist playing through tinny speakers in the background. His boots scuffed lightly against the concrete floor as he leaned forward to grab some ribbon, careful not to look at her directly. The air between them hadn't softened since they started wrapping. If anything, the tension grew sharper by the minute, like a wire ready to snap.

Across from him, Alexis' movements stayed sharp, quick. She barely paused, each gift another task to complete as if the faster she finished, the faster she could leave. Her phone buzzed every few minutes on the table next to her, but she ignored it for the most part, though not without a few flickers of irritation each time the screen lit up.

Brett squinted at his phone, replying to a text that didn't matter nearly as much as Alexis thought it did. He caught her staring at him when he put it away, her lips pressed into a thin line.

"Are you going to wrap anything, or just sit there and text?" She tossed the question like she tossed the tape across the table — sharp, pointed, and impossible to miss.

He let out a quiet sigh, reaching for another roll of red tartan paper. "I'm here, aren't I? Relax. We've got time."

Her jaw tightened, and for a moment, Brett regretted the calm tone. She might not admit it, but she wanted to be anywhere but here. He could feel it in every hurried movement, every time she glanced at her phone like a lifeline back to San Antonio.

"Maybe you've got time," she finally snapped, tearing off a piece of tape, "but I have work to do."

He frowned, watching her hands work faster, nearly shredding the white paper in her haste.

"Work, huh? You mean parties in San Antonio?"

The edge in her voice cut through the warmth of the Christmas carols playing in the background. "Yes. Parties in San Antonio. Some of us have businesses to run."

Her words hit harder than they should've. His fingers slowed on the ribbon, and he forced himself to keep tying the silver bow instead of answering right away. "You're not the only one with work, you know." He flicked a glance at her, but her eyes stayed fixed on the gift she wrapped. "Not everything revolves around parties."

Her sharp inhale filled the quiet between them, louder than the wrapping paper rustling in their hands. "You haven't had a client in weeks."

That stung. He fought to keep his expression calm, focusing on the ribbon, which suddenly seemed a lot more interesting. "If that's what you think, then I guess you haven't been paying attention."

She didn't respond immediately, but he felt the tension ripple through the space between them. Silence stretched, the only sounds coming from their hands moving over boxes and paper. And the occasional tenor notes from singing along with the Christmas carols under his breath. Each second seemed to deepen the space between them, like an invisible canyon they'd been staring at for months but never crossed.

Brett shifted in his seat, forcing his attention back to the wrapping. Every crinkle of paper, every snip of scissors reminded him how far apart they felt despite sitting just a few feet from each other. Her world, full of fancy parties and client meetings, seemed miles away from his — full of quiet projects he hadn't shared and a loneliness he wasn't ready to admit. And yet, here they were, brought together by some Christmas task the judge assigned, pretending to care about wrapping presents when everything else he left unsaid.

Another buzz from his phone snapped him out of his thoughts. He glanced at the screen, his lips twitching slightly at the message, but before he could reply, the door swung open, and Judge Henry strolled in.

"Ah, there you two are!" His voice boomed through the room, cheerful as ever, completely unaware of the tension thickening between them. He carried a large box under one arm, his usual smirk in place as he made his way to the table.

Alexis straightened, her hands still on the white wrapping paper. Brett glanced at her, catching the brief flash of annoyance on her face. The judge seemed to thrive on this kind of chaos, knowing exactly how to push their buttons without even trying.

"I've got one last present for you two to wrap," the judge said, dropping the box onto the table with a thud that made the paper tremble. "And when you're done with that, I'll need you both bright and early at Town Hall tomorrow. The mayor's got something special planned."

Brett exchanged a look with Alexis.

The mayor? Special plans? That rarely turned out well.

Brett pushed back from the table. "Special, huh?" With arms crossed loosely, he leaned back as he eyed the judge. "What kind of special are we talking about?"

The judge just grinned, leaning forward with a mischievous glint in his eye. "Wouldn't want to spoil the surprise."

A groan slipped out of Brett's mouth before he could stop it. "Surprises from the mayor usually mean trouble."

The judge winked. "Just make sure you're there. Bright and early. And by the way, Hazel and Harriet will be picking up all the gifts you've managed to wrap soon, so finish up, they don't like to be kept waiting." And with a final nod, he turned and left, the door clicking shut behind him, leaving them alone once again.

Alexis let out a long breath, the kind that said she wanted no more with this day as he did. Her fingers lingered on the edge of the box the judge had left, tracing the corners absently. "The mayor, huh? What do you think this 'special plan' is?"

Brett stood, stretching his back, feeling the slight tension ease as he did. "If I had to guess? Something ridiculous. Probably a costume."

Alexis shot him a look, one eyebrow arching in disbelief. "You think he's going to dress up?"

Brett chuckled, gathering some loose ribbon from the table. "You've met the guy, right? Of course, he's going to dress up."

They worked in silence for a few minutes, each of them focused on finishing the last few presents. But the weight of their earlier argument still hung in the air, heavy and unspoken. He glanced at her again. He noticed the way her shoulders had tensed, the way her fingers moved quicker now, as if she raced to finish and get out of there.

Her phone buzzed again, and this time, she picked it up, scanning the screen before quickly pocketing it. Brett watched her, curiosity creeping in. He wondered what kind of world she longed to escape back to with every text, what conversations were pulling her attention away. But asking would only start another argument.

Instead, he grabbed the last gift and started wrapping. The metallic gold paper slid between his fingers as he wrestled the package into place. The judge's surprise weighed in the back of his mind, but more than that, he wondered if anything remained of the ease they used to have with each other. Before Whiskey, before San Antonio.

The present nearly slipped from his hands as he tied the red bow around the last package. He laughed under his breath. "Well, whatever the mayor's got planned, it probably won't top the weirdness of today."

Alexis shook her head, a small smile tugging at her lips despite the tension still lingering. "I wouldn't bet on it."

As they finished wrapping the last boxes, Brett watched her from the corner of his eye. Even in the middle of this mess, with all the frustration bubbling beneath the surface, there's something about her — something that hadn't changed. That focus, that drive, the way she commanded any room she took part in.

These thoughts of her wrangled his concentration. Did she realize how much he still admired that about her, despite everything.

"Tomorrow at Town Hall," he said, breaking the silence as he stepped toward the door. "Don't be late."

Her eyes rolled with a hint of a smile. "Like you've ever been on time to anything."

The playful jab caught him off guard, and for a moment, something warm tugged at the edges of his chest.

Maybe there's still something left between them — something worth holding onto.

He wasn't sure yet. But even though he still had some doubts, he wouldn't let it go either.

He laughed as he pulled on his green down vest. He tossed her a glance. His lips ticked upward at one corner before his reply slipped past his lips. "Well,

Darlin if I can remember one particular date I wasn't late."

Alexis' brow rose. "Oh please do share."

"If you can remember about 5 years ago, I made it to our wedding on time."

Alexis froze with these words. Her brown eyes twinkled. She bit down on her bottom lip and nodded.

Brett picked up his brown Stetson, placed it on his head, then tapped the brim. He left the shelter, boots crunching through the snow against the gravel. Images flooded his memory of that day — her dress, the beauty she radiated, the music, the food, and the vows.

Until death do us part.

He blew out his breath, kept walking toward his truck where he managed to shake off the bitter sweetness that had now become his life for the past five years. And before he climbed into his truck, a large white passenger van with 'Whiskey Antiquers' plastered all over the vehicle pulled into the shelter. He watched Hazel and Harriet climb out and wave to him before they rushed inside.

He chuckled. "Now there's two crazy birds."

As he started up his truck, he couldn't help but thinking about the chaos the mayor had in store for them tomorrow. But as he pulled away from the shelter, his thoughts drifted back to Alexis and the way she'd glanced at her phone. Frustration bubbled just below her surface.

The judge had said tomorrow would be a surprise. But for Brett, the real surprise might be figuring out what came next — between him and Alexis, between the life they'd left behind and the one that still lingered, waiting to be decided.

FROM: The Whiskey Tattler Editors
TO: Whiskey Tattler Subscribers
CC:
Date: December 20th 3:22 pm CST
Subject: All wrapped up in Love...

THE WHISKEY TATTLER

Cowboy Heat & Gift Wrap Meltdown
By Hazel Montgomery
Deed Watch: Day Number 8
Task: Wrapping it up, or not?

Well, they're back at the Whiskey Salvation Shelter, not decorating cookies this time, but wrapping Christmas presents — and, oh, was there some unexpected sizzle in the air! No mistletoe, no Santa suits, but our Mr. Cowboy sure turned heads. Apparently, jeans and flannel does make a heart pitter patter is just as effective at sparking interest by the fireplace. Okay, so maybe more our hearts pitter pattered, but that just proves we're not dead!

The Heat Is On:

His denim shirt and cowboy hat combo? Not just calendar-material—it's wrapping-morale material, too.

Mrs. Claus—excuse me, our resident Mrs. Santa—looked perpetually Grinch-y. Serious, precise, all business... not exactly the holiday cheer we expect from someone who dresses in red velvet the other day!
I caught her muttering, "If he sings country Christmas carols one more time..."—but let's face it, the cowboy crooning is half the point.

Gift Wrap Rundown:

• 25 packages wrapped—ranging from fragile antiques to oversized board games.
• Several bows were tied with more affection than the couple's last three public outings combined.
• Tissue paper choices? He went bold: red tartan and metallic gold. Her? Plain white—because "color distracts from the craftsmanship,"

Honestly? The contrast was... amusing. He's whispering sweet country lyrics to a box; she's double-checking tape placement like a judge in a court procedure.

Just when the mood threatened to stay frosty, in strides Judge Henry — and clipboard in hand. He paused, sniffed the air (could be cinnamon), and said:
"Love the country flair, Brett. And those gifts? Deed 9 will go down as a treat —handing them out tomorrow."

A nod from His Honor means tomorrow we'll see our couple handing these beautifully wrapped treasures out tomorrow with the help of our own jolly big red. At least we think. And if the cowboy swagger sticks around, maybe — just maybe — this Mrs. Claus will crack a smile... but hey, we've been wrong before. So stay tuned.

Odds are 3 to 5 she does.
1 to 5 she doesn't.

Let's hope wrapping warms them up, because tomorrow's deed 10, present giveaway is where the real firework—or frost—might begin.

Stay tuned, holiday spies.

Hazel Montgomery,

Co-Editor of the Whiskey Tattler and your ever-observant twin correspondent

Chrissy Hartmann

Chapter 13

December 21st

Deed Day Number 9

Christmas music echoed through the lobby of City Hall, accompanied by the shrill squeals of children darting around, chasing one another through the maze of decorated trees and oversized candy canes. Alexis pulled her scarf tighter around her neck, half-jogging through the entrance, her heels clicking loudly against the polished floor. Late again. Not by much, but enough to leave her stomach in knots.

Brett better not have bailed on me already.

Huffing a breath, she scanned the crowd, looking for a familiar face among the chaos. Mothers wrangled toddlers, babies tugged at Santa hats, and somewhere in the midst of it all, the mayor would make his supposed grand entrance as Santa. All part of the ridiculous deed the judge had cooked up for them.

Elves. Really? Elves.

Not exactly what she envisioned when she thought of ways to save her marriage.

Alexis straightened, searching the room. Still no sign of Brett. Of course. Typical. Probably off with that woman, the one she'd seen him talking to at the Christmas tea. *Work? Right. IF that's what he wants to call it. Ha!*

He'd been spending more time at his workshop, hadn't he? Always "fixing things," always keeping busy, as if he cared only about work. Not her. Not them. The ache in her chest swelled. A mother waved frantically in her direction. "Miss! Can you help me get little Billy to Santa? He won't stop squirming!"

Help? Her? Not exactly. Not yet. Alexis forced a smile, holding up a hand to stall the woman. "Give me a second." Her eyes darted to the mayor's oversized Santa throne, surrounded by a crowd of children, all jockeying for position. The man in red, cheeks flushed and white beard slightly askew, clapped his hands together with practiced enthusiasm.

"Alexis!" The mayor boomed, cutting through the noise. "Come on, join the party! We've got plenty of kids waiting for Santa's helpers to show up!"

Show up.

That stung. "Where's Brett?" She forced herself to sound neutral, even as irritation prickled under her skin.

Late, like always. Or gone.

The mayor laughed, pointing to the far end of the room. "Oh, he's here, alright. Right on time, too. Take a look."

Alexis turned, expecting to see Brett in his usual jeans and flannel. Her eyes widened. Not jeans. Not flannel. An elf costume, complete with striped tights, a green tunic with a triangular-shaped collar, and a hat that flopped comically to the side with bells. Brett, her stoic, unflappable husband, looked like he'd walked straight out of a Christmas pageant — one he definitely had no business being in. Laughter bubbled up before she could stop it. It burst out, spilling over as Brett caught sight of her, his expression unreadable except for the faintest lift of his brow. Alexis doubled over, clutching her stomach as the absurdity of it all hit her like a jolt of holiday cheer. The kids running around, the mayor in his wobbly Santa getup, and now Brett — Mr. Serious Carpenter — dressed as the world's tallest elf.

He crossed the room in long, purposeful strides, somehow managing to look dignified despite the ridiculous costume. Alexis wiped at her eyes. He stopped and placed his hands on his hips. He grinned as if she looked out of place.

"Nice outfit." She couldn't resist. "Bet you'll be the talk of the town."

Brett glanced down at his pointed shoes, then back up. "Thought you weren't gonna show." His voice carried the same low rumble it always had, but something in his eyes softened, just for a moment. Maybe she imagined it. Maybe she wanted to imagine it.

Alexis shook her head, the remnants of her laughter still hanging in the air between them. "Wouldn't miss this for the world." Her gaze swept over him again. With fingers splayed over her lips trying to hold back the laughter. "Really pulling off the whole elf thing. Very... festive."

Brett smirked. The corners of his mouth twitched, but he held his ground. "You're late."

"Again, you noticed." Alexis crossed her arms, leaning back on one heel. "Where's my costume?"

Mayor Dymblebee materialized beside them, clapping his hands together with a grin as wide as Texas. "Oh, it's in the back! Didn't think you'd mind, Mrs. Stapleton, seeing as how you're a bit of a social butterfly." His eyes twinkled with a mix of mischief and holiday spirit. "You and Brett here are gonna be the best elves this town's ever seen."

The best elves?

Alexis held back another laugh, glancing at Brett, who stood with his arms crossed, looking like he'd rather be anywhere else. But he'd come. And that counted for something, didn't it?

"Guess I'll go change." She turned toward the back room tossing a last look at Brett. The elf hat flopped again as he shifted, his eyes meeting hers in that steady, unwavering way of his. Something inside her twisted. Something she'd not felt in a long time. A familiar warmth of something mixed with confusion. She hesitated, just for a second. Why did he come? Not just physically, but really here, putting up with this insanity. For the first time in a long time, she couldn't brush him off as the absent husband, always working, always somewhere else.

Brett watched her, silent, stoic as ever, but his presence felt like a challenge. He didn't say anything, just waited, like he always did, as if he knew she'd come to him when ready.

Alexis bit her lip, the laughter gone now, replaced by a tug of something deeper. She slipped through the door, heading toward the costume room, but her mind lingered on him.

Had he changed? The question gnawed at her as she pulled the elf costume off its hanger. Brett didn't do things halfway. Never had. If he didn't care, if he didn't still love her on some level, why would he bother showing up? The Brett she knew didn't waste time on things he didn't believe in. And this... this to most would be nothing but ridiculous. A sacrifice of pride if nothing else. Maybe he had changed. Or maybe she just wanted him to.

She slipped into the striped tights, her mind racing. Five years. Five years of feeling like she always pushed, always asking for more than he could give. But now, standing in a back room surrounded by elf costumes and candy canes, she wondered. Had she been pushing him away the whole time? Or had they both just stopped trying?

She smoothed the tunic down over her hips, glancing in the mirror. Ridiculous. But at least now she matched Brett. The thought made her smile again.

If he didn't still love her, why would he go along with this? Why put up with the crazy list of deeds the judge had thrown at them, when it would've been so much easier to walk away?

Alexis twisted the floppy elf hat onto her head, then took a deep breath. Maybe it wasn't just about the deeds. Maybe it could only be about them. About what they still had, buried under years of misunderstandings and silence. She pushed the door open, stepping back into the chaotic lobby, ready to face whatever came next — with Brett by her side, whether she liked it or not.

The mayor clapped his hands again as she walked out the door signaling the start of their elf duties. "Now let's look Wonderful, you two! Absolutely perfect." His voice boomed, carrying that unrelenting cheer. "I know you both will be the best elves I've ever had. You'll make a wonderful team!"

Brett shot Alexis a sideways glance. "Yeah. Wonderful team."

She met his gaze, and something unspoken passed between them — an acknowledgment of the absurdity, maybe. Or perhaps just relief that in a few hours they'd have another deed crossed off the list.

"Well," the mayor adjusted his belt on the Santa suit. "The kids are all set to start, but there's one more thing we need to do."

Brett crossed his arms, a wary expression growing on his face. "What's that?"

"Well," the mayor glanced over his shoulder as the door opened. Judge Henry strolled in, his presence commanding but his face full of mischief. "The town's live nativity scene needs help tomorrow and guess who volunteered you?"

The mayor beamed.

Brett groaned rubbing the back of his neck, while Alexis' mouth dropped open. "You're kidding."

"I'm very serious," Judge Henry nodded with finality. "We're going to need extra hands, and well, you two fit the bill. But first — " He stepped back, reaching into his pocket and pulling out a camera. "How about a little picture for the memories?"

FROM: The Whiskey Tattler Editors
TO: Whiskey Tattler Subscribers
CC:
BCC:
Date: December 21st 11:44 am CST
Subject: Elfing it up...

THE WHISKEY TATTLER

Elf Ensembles & Cowboy Charm
By Hazel and Harriet Montgomery
Deed Watch: Day Number 10
Task: It's all about the Elf

Hazel Speaks:

Well, peppers! Our intrepid duo showed up yesterday donning full Santa-elf attire—tall hats, pointy ears, stripes, bells—the whole workshop ensemble. And guess who stole the show? Mr. Cowboy himself, stepping out in those elf stockings with such gusto he left more than a few onlookers gawking.

One local — Mrs. Jenkins from Maple Lane — shook her head and said:
"He looked positively adorable — like the rugged Christmas card we didn't know we needed!"

Take that, Mrs. Claus-seriousness.

Harriet Inserts Snark:

Grinning or grimacing? The judge was overheard muttering as he snapped a photo (he always tries for the exclusive):
"If these stockings get more attention than my courtroom robe, I'll be filing a complaint!"

He's not wrong—but the town's excited, and even the mayor managed to sneak in for a snap-worthy moment. One cheerful passerby noted:
"It was adorable — the mayor as Santa got in on the fun for a photo op too. I haven't seen him smile like that since last year's pecan pie contest!"

Cowboy Looks in Elf Stockings:

That denim cowboy just worked the stripes—more rugged meets whimsical.

Chrissy Hartmann

Mrs. Claus (ahem, Mrs. Santa-elf) stayed stiff as ever. Serious tape-measure vibes around the gift-wrap table, bless her.

Contrast couldn't be sharper:
him, playfully crooked stockings; her, positively prim.

Judge Henry's Final Word:
Before departing, the Judge leaned in with clipboard in hand and teased, "you all look fantastic — and tomorrow's deed 10? No stockings, but maybe a little nativity creativity is needed."

Of course that had our brows rising like the Texas sun. Hmm?

So, there you have it. No kisses yet, but defin-itely heat. The elf stockings have legged it into town legend. And the mayor? Smiling. And us? Plotting.

Signed, with a jingling flair,

Hazel and Harriet Montgomery

Twins, Editors of the Whiskey Tattler, and Elfing Around
Since 1945

Chapter 14

December 22nd
Deed Day Number 10
Brett's boots sank into the muddy ground, the earth clinging to his steps as the sun hovered low in the sky. He straightened from where he'd been adjusting the wooden manger and glanced across the makeshift barn. The hay scattered beneath the animals carried a musty, earthy scent, mingling with the faint aroma of pine trees strung with lights around the churchyard. Alexis, busy at the other end of the pen, brushed her hands off after organizing the decorations.

She moved with the kind of energy that always left him awed and uneasy. Every flicker of her hand, every step she took, so sure of herself. He forced his gaze back to the task in front of him.

Stay focused.

He adjusted the wooden stable frame again to ensure it wouldn't collapse under the weight of the decorations. His fingers, rough and calloused, gripped the wood with the kind of care he reserved for his projects. Building things, that's what he understood.

Alexis' laugh drifted toward him, carried by the cold breeze caught him off guard. He peeked in her direction. Her face glowed in the warm light of the decorations with eyes twinkling mischievously as she teased one of the volunteers. She had a way of drawing people in, making them feel like they belonged.

Brett's gut twisted, not from the cold, but from something deeper, something he couldn't shake. That had been part of their problem, hadn't it?

She craved connection. He craved solitude.

Children's laughter erupted near the nativity scene, breaking his thoughts. Brett watched as Alexis crouched down to help one of the kids adjust a sheep costume. Her voice carried the perfect blend of patience and charm, and for a second, he found himself envying those kids. The way she gave them attention — the sort of attention he no longer got.

The thought crawled into his chest and settled like an old fire bruised anvil.

With the daylight fading into night, he dusted off his hands on his jeans. Then securing his hat, he headed toward her.

The air snapped with cold.

Brett reached for the live donkey's reins. "You need help?" His voice a little gruff. He glanced at Alexis sideways. She raised an eyebrow, but her smile softened whatever barrier had been there.

"Yeah, thanks." She handed him the end of the rope. Her fingers brushing his for the briefest second.

His pulse kicked up. And not wanting to show its affect, he acted as if nothing had happened. But his insides would say different.

Not allowing his heart to take over, he moved the donkey toward the enclosure.

Okay, get a grip. Just the brush of fingers. Nothing else.

He led the animal without any unnecessary tugging. Steady, controlled.

The crowd started to drift away. The event winding down. Lights twinkled against the backdrop of the town's main street. Brett looked around. He took in the scene — families huddled together, hot cocoa and coffee steaming in their hands, the chatter of conversation fading into the background like the hum of bees. This time of the year, always carried a quiet sense of magic. But tonight? With Alexis standing near, well, it also carried a strange tightness in his chest. His heart gave a little extra kick.

Brett tried to shake it off. But the sensation wouldn't go away.

Hmm?

Not sure what to do, he told his ticker to calm down.

Not the time or place for that right now.

But instead, his heart replied back with another quick thump.

Brett growled at himself.

Not noticing Brett's argument with his heart, she leaned against the gate. Her hair slightly damp from the mist, framed her face. She caught him looking and smiled. A weary, knowing smile. "You didn't have to do all this, you know." No accusation, just a statement.

He tightened the rope around the gatepost. "Didn't mind."

And in all actuality, he hadn't minded at all, really. If anything, being here, helping her, it gave him a sense of closeness he hadn't expected.

He inhaled sharply, the crisp scent of pine and chilly air filled his lungs. The attempt made to steady his sudden rush of unease.

The clang of boots on gravel announced the arrival of someone else. Brett turned just in time to see the judge walking toward them. The man's stride quick and steady despite his age. He always seemed to appear when you least expected it with an ornery glint in his eye — like he knew something you didn't.

Brett straightened with tensed muscles.

Judge Henry's gruff gravelly voice broke through the quiet lull of the evening. "Well, now, looks like you two pulled off another miracle." He nodded toward the nativity, then fixed both of them with a gaze that seemed to cut through any pretense.

Brett shifted on his feet, but said nothing.

Alexis, however, pushed herself off the gate and crossed her arms. A small smile played at her lips. "It wasn't so bad. The kids enjoyed it."

The judge chuckled. "That they did. But I didn't come here just to tell you that." His hands disappeared into the pockets of his thick coat. His expression turned sly. "Tomorrow, you'll both be helping a group of kids at Beans and Leaves coffee shoppe for some Christmas caroling."

Brett's brow furrowed. "Caroling?" The word came out slow, like he needed to process it before he could fully accept it.

"Yup. But there's a catch." The judge grinned. The kind of smile that meant trouble. "I'll tell you the twist tomorrow. Get some rest. You'll need it." And with that, he tipped his hat and strode off toward

Beans and Leaves. Boots crunching on the frosty ground.

Brett turned to Alexis. His stomach tightened. His mind wrapped around the judge's cryptic message. He raised a brow in Alexis' direction. "Now what do ya think that's all about?"

She shrugged, though her eyes gleamed with curiosity. "Who knows? The man always has some sort of motive." A hint of a smile peaked at the corner of her mouth. "He loves keeping us on our toes."

Brett rubbed the back of his neck, an old habit whenever uncertainty struck. The judge's words, the deeds they had been completing — each task had drawn them together in ways he hadn't expected. Being with her, even when they weren't talking, even when the distance between them still felt wide — it made him want to close that gap. And yet, the finish line stretched out before them, looming just around the corner. Twelve deeds, with only two to go. Then they'd be done. Divorce granted.

His chest tightened again. His ticker kicked an odd pattern he couldn't shake. This day, the next, it all lead to an end. But would it be the one he wanted?

Not able to traverse that trail of thoughts, he pushed it back — way back into his thoughts.

The movement of Alexis gathering the rest of the decorations made him want to say something. But the tiredness she exhibited with her slower movements and longer pauses brought out a resistance to unload on her just exactly how he felt.

She started to adjust the lights, but paused only to look up at him. But it lasted only a second, as if she sensed the unspoken tension between them.

He stood still. Said nothing. Just watched.

Alexis sighed, looked at the lights as if she spoke to them. Then lifting her head, she glanced at Brett.

"Guess we'll see what he throws at us next." Her voice held a lightness he envied, like she could brush off the weight of this whole thing without breaking stride.

With mental hogties, he tied down his emotions and bent to help her with the lights.

Just focus on the lights. Nothing else. Not her hands. Not those eyes. And definitely not those lips. Just focus.

But telling himself to focus on the work wasn't the easiest thing to do. Not especially with the only woman he ever loved stood next to him. In fact, he could smell the peppermint in her hair.

While he rolled the extra set of lights into a loop, he wanted nothing, but to use the twinklers to rope Alexis into him. He wouldn't though. Not because people would talk, hell, he could care less about that.

But only because Alexis didn't want him to. She agreed to these twelve deeds for the divorce. And him? Well, sure he went along with it, but what else could he do? He'd already hurt her enough, he had no intention of doing it again.

But the way their silence felt so... familiar it made his heart ache. He took his coil of lights and tossed them into a crate.

The night deepened around them. The stars started to pierce through the clouds, faint but steady.

He glanced around. A few clumps of hay lay scattered where the manger laid. He gathered the last of the snow-tromped hay. The coldness tightened the muscles in his hands with his breath hanging in the air.

Alexis stood a foot away. Her arms wrapped around herself, though whether from the chill or from something deeper, he couldn't tell.

In the quiet, with the world settling down around them, the gap between them felt less like a divide and more like a silk thread — thin, fragile, but still there. How many more deeds would they complete together before the thread snapped?

The cold bit into his skin, but Brett barely noticed. As he untied the last knot on the gate, his mind turned to tomorrow, to what the judge had planned, and more importantly, to what would come after.

Is this what it's left to? Fleeting moments? Moments slipping away? Ones I can't corral? Or is there even something worth holding onto?

A horn honked. Brett turned to watch the judge drive past with a wave. "Hmm?"

Maybe it's going to take all twelve of these crazy deeds to figure this out. Maybe old Judge Henry might be on to something.

He shook his head and chuckled.

Well... maybe.

FROM: The Whiskey Tattler Editors
TO: Whiskey Tattler Subscribers
CC:
Date: December 22nd 9:15 pm CST
Subject: No Kiss, no hot cocoa, what the?

THE WHISKEY TATTLER

Nativity Debacle & Near-Miss Sparks
By Hazel and Harriet Montgomery,
Deed Watch: Day Number 11
Task: Nativity Creativity

Hazel's Melodrama:
Darlings, deed 10 started with our couple and a trip over
to the Whiskey Salvation Shelter's nativity. Peaceful,
right? Ha! Think innocent songs and marshmallow
mountains...until the nativity setup tumbled. A shepherd's
staff smacked the baby Jesus figurine, an angelic foghorn
(someone thought fog machine!) went off, and suddenly
you had aliens, snowmen and 5 of the weirdest nativity
chaos levels — no exaggeration! Well, maybe a little.

Harriet's Mayhem Analysis:
Well, not exactly, but... Watch your mistletoe, folks —
witnesses say there might have been a kiss at the end of the
night. He reached to secure some twinkle lights, she
wrangled the donkey reigns for him ...then paused. A
spark—clearly visible under the streetlights and stars! But
alas, no smooch. Instead, he shrugged and asked if she
wanted a hot cocoa. Eyes locked. Hearts may have
fluttered. Okay, okay, no hot chocolate moment, but there
should have been one.

Meanwhile, the manger's donation box was thriving: —
Charities donated tallied $240 for better security.
— plus $45 in hay donations. Town's feeling warm in more
ways than one.

What's Next?
Deed 11 — Hot cocoa and caroling from angels on high
with plenty of marshmallows!

Signing with marshmallow love,

Hazel and Harriet Montgomery,

Twins, Editors of the Whiskey Tattler, and your on-the-spot nativity chroniclers

Chrissy Hartmann

Chapter 15

December 23rd
Deed Day Number 11

The rich, harmonious voices of the Methodist children's church choir filled the coffee shoppe, their final rendition of "Silent Night" wrapping the room in soft melody. Alexis stood behind the makeshift cocoa stand created especially for the kidders tapping her fingers to the rhythm. She kept her eyes on the preteens as they sang, the joy in their faces reminding her of the reason for this chaotic fundraiser. Yet, her gaze drifted to Brett. The man stood stationed beside the hot cocoa dispensers. He dutifully poured drinks with steady hands.

He hadn't sung a single note all evening, just like she had expected. His silence hung between them, as always. Even as he served cup after cup of cocoa with that familiar intensity — the unspoken divide lingered.

She turned toward him, watching how his focus never wavered, how his hands worked with the same precision he brought to his carpentry. Her fingers itched to nudge him, to break the routine they had slipped into. The man didn't sing, didn't talk unless necessary, and yet, every once in a while, she caught glimpses of the man she had fallen for — the one who hadn't always been so locked away. The thought lingered as she handed a cup to a little rosy-cheeked girl in a Santa hat.

The young choir's harmony echoed against the tables and booths. It danced between the smell of chocolate and peppermint. The warmth of the hot cocoa stand fought back the cold that seeped in through the front door. But Alexis' heart remained unsettled — A contrast to the festive surroundings. Her body swayed slightly to the song's final verse, but the tension in her chest grew. She looked at Brett again, frustration building in her throat.

The choir finished, and applause rippled through the small crowd that had gathered to listen. Alexis let out a breath, then shot a glance toward the corner booth across the shoppe where Hazel and Harriet sat, selling tickets for the upcoming Christmas dance. Those two women, who unofficially ran half the town, observed the scene with skeptical eyes, probably plotting something, as they always did.

Brett handed out another cup, steam rising from the cocoa in the chilled air of the coffee shoppe. His posture remained rigid, like he could endure the entire night without cracking a smile or softening his stance. She bit her lip. Her frustration bloomed into something vulnerable. Something raw. "Enjoying yourself over there?" Alexis leaned closer, placing her hand on the counter between them, her voice low enough to stay unnoticed by the straggling customers.

Brett glanced at her. His eyes lingered for a second longer than usual. "Serving cocoa." He spoke with no hint of playfulness, but his response hadn't been harsh either.

She sighed inwardly, the familiar dance of their distance playing out again. She tilted her head as her gaze wandered over the quieting shoppe. The twinkling Christmas lights reflected off the tables and front window casting a glow that somehow made everything feel more intimate. The warm smell of cocoa and freshly baked bread surrounded them. But the weight of unspoken words hung heavier. A shiver ran through her. Not that noticeable, after all, the coffee shoppe's revolving door allowed for a gust of frigid wind to sneak in. She crossed her arms, turning her body toward Brett. The song had ended, the preteens were busy packing up their sheet music, and soon it would just be them here. Alone, for what felt like the hundredth time. With one step, she leaned into him as he bent to pour the last hot cocoa. "You're always so serious."

Unsure he heard her through the church choir's cleanup and the bustle of last-minute shoppers, she leaned even closer. But Brett's hand paused in mid-pour. His back stiffened only for a second before he straightened. He set the cocoa pot back on the burner. His shoulders dropping just a fraction. "Just trying to help."

She brushed up against him, her pulse quickening despite herself. The space between them had never felt so small, yet so enormous. "We're supposed to be doing these deeds together." Her tone soft but edged with the same ache she had been carrying since they'd started this ridiculous process. "That's what the judge wanted."

And maybe... Maybe I want that too.

Brett's eyes met hers, finally, really met them. His hand, still gripping the handle of the cocoa dispenser, loosened. He didn't move closer, didn't say anything, but something in the way he looked at her softened the sharpness between them.

Alexis glanced down at the counter suddenly unsure of where to go next. Her heart raced. The silence grew louder around them with a different kind of tension building between them. If she just leaned in, just reached out —

A burst of laughter shattered the moment. Hazel and Harriet waddled over from their corner booth, their bright scarves fluttering as they approached. "Well, look at this, Harriet ." Hazel grinned. "Santa's little helpers look like they're up to more than cocoa!"

Brett jerked back, his hand dropping from the counter as though he had been caught doing something wrong.

Alexis cursed the timing under her breath, her pulse still racing from how close they had been. "We were just talking." Alexis stepped away from BRETT, pasting on a smile, though her heart pounded in her chest.

Harriet, her eyes twinkling with mischief, waved off Alexis' response. "Oh, honey, no need to explain. We've had our fair share of romances to recognize when two people are 'just talking."

Brett cleared his throat, running a hand over the back of his neck.

Alexis glanced at him from the corner of her eye, the tension still simmering just below the surface. Not wanting to stir up any more dust, Brett moved closer to the two older ladies, but only to distract them. "What's going on?"

"Well," Hazel began, clasping her hands together in front of her, "Judge H has a little message for you both."

Alexis' stomach dropped. Another message from the judge. She could already tell this wasn't going to be a simple update.

"You two are going to be helping us out at the Christmas Eve ball tomorrow night," Hazel continued, her smile widening. "Serving drinks. Same deal as tonight, only with more... spirit, if you catch my meaning." She winked, her laugh as rich as the cocoa they had been serving.

Harriet chuckled and leaned in closer. "Judge said he'll be there too, with a little 'discussion' about your... situation. But don't worry, Santa will be watching. And I'm sure he'll bring the both of you what you really want for Christmas." She tapped the side of her nose.

Brett's jaw tightened.

Alexis shot him a quick glance. Again, the tension surfaced — that tension, that unresolved knot between them that just kept tightening with each passing day of these twelve deeds. She frowned noticing his hands were now buried in his pockets. His usual stance when he felt cornered.

Alexis forced a smile, though her mind raced. "Sounds... great."

Hazel's eyes sparkled behind her cat rimmed glasses. "It'll be a night to remember, mark my words. And maybe, just maybe, Santa will have a special gift for you two."

Harriet waved her hand, as if brushing off the implication. "Oh, don't go scaring them off, Hazel. They're just doing the judge's bidding, after all." She winked at Alexis, her words holding layers of meaning she wasn't entirely prepared to unpack.

As the two old women strolled back to their booth, giggling like schoolgirls, Alexis let out a slow breath. The tension in her shoulders remained, though now it mingled with something else — something more urgent. The judge, the dance, the twelve deeds...

where could all of this be heading?

Brett remained silent beside her, his gaze distant.

She looked at him, studying the way his brow furrowed, the way his hands stayed deep in his pockets as if he were trying to hide the weight of everything they weren't saying. With her voice barely above a whisper, Alexis leaned closer. "Are we really just going to serve drinks tomorrow?"

His eyes slid to hers, the softness from earlier gone, replaced by the guarded expression she had come to know so well. "We'll find out, won't we?"

His voice, as quiet as hers, hung between them, but this time the tension had shifted — something else lingered between them. Something unspoken, something they had danced around for days now.

Alexis looked away. Her own kind of pressure building in her chest again, the same question circling in her mind.

If they we're completing these deeds just to end it all with a divorce, why did being near him still feel so complicated, so... unfinished?

She turned back to the cocoa stand and tidied up the last of the supplies. Brett moved beside her, helping without a word. His presence steady, but distant. Tomorrow loomed large in her mind, the dance, the judge's discussion, and whatever gift Hazel and Harriet hinted at. It all swirled together.

And in the fading noise of the Beans and Leaves Coffee Shoppe, with the last notes of Christmas carols still echoing in the background, Alexis' thoughts couldn't escape one question.

What if the ending we're heading toward isn't the one I really want?

FROM: The Whiskey Tattler Editors
TO: Whiskey Tattler Subscribers
CC:
Date: December 23rd 8:43 pm CST
Subject: A Marshmallow Kind of Love

THE WHISKEY TATTLER

Choir Chaperoning & Cocoa Heat
By Hazel and Harriet Montgomery
Deed Watch: Day Number 11
Task: It's not all about the Marshmallows

Found our intrepid couple, Brett and Alexis Stapleton doubling as chaperones for the Methodist youth choir — inside Beans and Leaves Coffee Shoppe, no less — while managing the hot cocoa stand for charity. And let me tell you, things got steamy in more ways than one.

Choir Chaos:

Little voices floated over the tables of people — "Silent Night" one moment, "Jingle Bell Rock" the next—while coffee drinkers dodged Christmassy renditions between the colored marshmallow display and dessert case.

The kids were adorable, but as volume rose, so did the tension: the stock room became impromptu stage, complete with miniature conductors and several enthusiastic choir leaders.

Cocoa Stand Commotion:

Steamy mugs were flying — literal steam rising from the cocoa like a cauldron of winter magic.

Our duo juggled marshmallows, caregivers, and choir kids eager for a sugar boost before their next verse.

We noted "the air was thick — in cocoa, carols, and maybe... something unspoken between our couple?"

Heat in the Air:

No mistletoe required—the combination of steamy cocoa, carols, and Styrofoam cups created its own romantic climate.
While no kiss was exchanged (kids within earshot), Harriet and I can both confirm they saw several

"intentional cocoa-top-sip-time" moments between them — those stolen glances said it all.

Onward to deed 12:

Tomorrow night brings the big finale at the Christmas Eve Ball, where our lovebirds will serve refreshments to the guests. If we Den Mothers, Hazel and Harriet have anything to say? Bring a fire extinguisher—because when mistletoe meets mood, things might just catch on fire.

Signed, steaming yet scandal-free,

Hazel and Harriet Montgomery

Twins, Editors of the Whiskey Tattler, and Your Hot Cocoa & Choir Chaperones

Chrissy Hartmann

Chapter 16

December 24th

The music began to fade as the last couples twirled around the dance floor. Laughter and conversation filled the room, but Brett could barely hear it. His focus stayed on the woman across from him at the bar. One very familiar toh him and an interior decorator, Serena Stapleton. And let's not forget to mention, his cousin. A woman, Alexis had never met. Well, she'd been introduced long ago. Maybe at a school event? Maybe at one of the family's BBQs? What wherever it had been, the scowl on Alexis' face made it clear to those around him she had no recollection and no idea who the woman might be.

Serena leaned in slightly, her red lips forming words that didn't fully register. He nodded absently, glancing over her shoulder to where Alexis stood at the far end of the room, her phone glowing in her hand.

Serena's voice broke through the haze. "We can start the renovations in January, get everything ready by spring. Maybe add some warmth with those colors we talked about?"

Brett shifted, his fingers grazing the rim of a glass on the counter. "Yeah, sounds good." He wasn't sure if it did, not really. The idea of redoing the house had started to feel more like a lifeline than a design project. Each stroke of paint, each piece of contemporary yet comfy furniture, all meant for Alexis. Meant to bring her back. But her face, illuminated by her phone as she scrolled through something on her screen, now became unreadable.

Across the bar, Alexis tucked a stray strand of hair behind her ear, her movements quick, impatient. The sleek cocktail dress she wore shimmered under the lights, every bit the life-of-the-party woman he had always admired and never understood. Tonight, though, she wasn't hosting, wasn't laughing. Her fingers moved faster on her phone, the irritation radiating off her in waves he could practically feel from across the bar.

Serena's eyes followed his gaze, her lips curving into a knowing smile. "She's still watching those events in San Antonio, huh? Big night for her business, I'd guess."

Brett's jaw tightened. "She's always watching something," he muttered, low enough to sound like he didn't mean to say it out loud.

Serena raised an eyebrow but said nothing.

She knew her role here — a yeah sure they were family, but at the moment, they were all professional, someone he hired to redecorate the space he wanted for Alexis. Nothing more. And anyway, Serena didn't like to medal. Wel, maybe sometimes. But with Brett and her return to the area after all these years, she needed the business, and no matter how much she'd like to speak her peace about Brett and the stupidity going on between he and his wife, she kept her mouth shut. Yet, every time he met with her, Alexis turned up to, and the space in his marriage stretched wider. And tonight, well, it felt like it might break wide open like the pastures on the horizon.

Alexis glanced over from her phone, catching Brett studying her with a sharpness that cut through the festive air. She moved toward him, setting her phone down on the counter beside her, no smile, no pretense of politeness. "Enjoying yourself?" Her voice slipped through the noise — sharp enough to sting.

Brett straightened. "Just talking about the house."

"That's what you're calling it?" She crossed her arms, the glow of the holiday lights reflecting off her skin, but nothing softened in her stance.

Brett watched as Serena shifted uncomfortably. Her smile now awkward, as if realizing she had walked into something far bigger than a design project. "I should... give you two a moment." She slid off her stool with a quick nod, turning and disappearing into the crowd.

Alexis waited until she'd left, her eyes never leaving Brett. "Really? This is how you spend your time while I'm making sure our business doesn't fall apart?"

The words Brett spoke next came through a clenched jaw. "It's your business. This isn't about that, Alexis. It's about us."

Alexis' scoffed at his words. Her eyes narrowed. "Oh, is it? Funny, because it sure looks like you're just fine without me. You and your little project."

The muscles in his chest tightened. The words came with a growl. "I'm trying to make things better. For you. For us."

The faint scent of Alexis' perfume drifted toward him drawing out memories he'd tried to bury long ago. "Better? You think a new coat of paint fixes this?" She waved her hand between them, her voice rising. "You think redoing the house changes the fact that you've spent the last five years acting like I'm invisible?"

White knuckling the bar with one hand, Brett dug his fingers into his palm to help keep himself from exploding. "It's not about the house. It's about trying."

The music faded away as if it were only them in the room.

Alexis stepped up to Brett. The space between them wouldn't allow a drink straw to pass. She jabbed him in the chest with a manicured index finger. "Trying?" Her voice trembled. "You only started trying when you realized I wanted no more. Now you want to play the hero and save everything with a renovation?" She jabbed him again. "It's too late."

The words hit like a punch, but he stood still, rooted in place by the weight of them.

Stay calm. Don't lose your control.

He relaxed his jaw. "It's not too late," He wrapped his free hand around hers that jabbed him. The softness of her hands sank into his calloused ones. He wanted nothing but to wrap her in his arms right now, but she wouldn't have it. So instead, he pulled her closer. Their lips almost touched. "Not if you don't want it to be."

Alexis' eyes flashed, tears threatening at the corners, but she blinked them back as she pulled her hand free from his. She pushed off him and stepped back. "Don't you dare put this on me. You want to save this? Then why couldn't you try before now? Why couldn't you see that I needed you to let me in?"

The music had vanished from the background completely now. The festive air now heavy with something neither of them wanted to face. Brett held up his hands. "I see it now. And I'm trying to — "

"No." Alexis cut him off, shaking her head. "You're too late." She grabbed her phone from the counter and scooped up her purse from a shelf under the bar.

Brett stood there stunned as he watched her walk away. The clicking of her heels resembling the click each time his revolver emptied a chamber. The distance between had once resembled miles, but now? Now a blackhole had opened up pulling his heart into its depth. With the finality in her words, Brett's Mind grappled for something to hold on to, but found nothing, making him helpless to follow.

Behind him, the soft shuffle of footsteps approached. The familiar sound of boots on the floor made him tense, but he didn't turn. Judge Henry broke the silence. "Well, that's a damn shame."

Brett swallowed hard, his throat tight. "I… I tried. I really did."

"Maybe so, But sometimes." The judge rubbed at his jaw. "Trying's not enough."

The room temperature dropped. The Christmas lights dimmed. And Brett's heart collapsed. He Closed his eyes dragging in his breath. His mind searched for a way to get back to the moment before everything had fallen apart.

Judge Henry crossed his arms, letting out a heavy breath. "You've got one more shot, son. We'll meet on the 26th. If things haven't changed by then..." He didn't finish the sentence, didn't need to.

The word "divorce" hung in the air, unspoken but solid, like an anvil ready to drop.

Too numb to respond, Brett nodded.

Judge Henry turned, but looked back over his shoulder, "Think long and hard about what you want, Brett. It's not just the house that needs fixing." And without another word, the judge left. The heavy thud of the door swung shut behind him echoing through the now quiet space.

Brett stared at the empty room, the twinkling lights mocking him. His hands clenched at his sides, loosened, but the weight on his chest remained. The party, the dance, the twelve deeds — none of it mattered now... Not if she walked away for good.

FROM: The Whiskey Tattler Editors
TO: Whiskey Tattler Subscribers
CC:
BCC:
Date: December 24th 11:31 pm CST
Subject: Bartending Bets

THE WHISKEY TATTLER

Bar Flair & Betrayal
By Hazel and Harriet Montgomery
Deed Watch: Day Number 12
Task: Last Call

Tonight's assignment?

Our couple donned full bartending regalia at the Christmas Eve Ball—shaking cocktails, pouring cheer, and slinging festive refreshments. But amid the tinsel and boot-scooting boogie, the cowboy's charm (AKA - Brett) may have lassoed trouble...

Flirt Metrics (Because We're That Snarky):

Situation Attempted Flirt % Actual Flirt Rate
Cowboy's Mystery Lady 87% (caffeine-addled judge of body language)   65% (winks, eye contact, light hand-touch possibility)

Ex's Reaction (eye-rolls/minutes glaring)   —   57% of the night

Yes, the cowboy pulled out his best bartender playbook—loud chuckles, intense eye contact, a well-timed "Here, let me fix your drink" — classic low-key flirting strategies bartenders swear by
And the ex? She was less "Christmas cheer" and more "cold shoulder" – we clocked her scowls faster than the wine refills.

Holiday Flair and Fire:

Refreshment specials were flying off the bar faster than Santa's sleigh—almost 120 served before midnight.
The cowboy looked like Mr. February part deux, albeit in a crisp white shirt, suspenders, and elf-level swagger.
But when he slid a peppermint martini to "that other lady," the Ex nearly ignited — ember-level warmth, not 'mistletoe' warm.

Chrissy Hartmann

Hazel and Harriet Montgomery predict: Tomorrow's Deed completed — the end of the night, packages handed out, and maybe, just maybe, fireworks (not the good kind).

Signed with sugar, sarcasm, and shaken-not-stirred skepticism,

Hazel and Harriet Montgomery

Twins, Editors of the Whiskey Tattler, and Your Cocktail-Craving Chroniclers

Chapter 17

December 25th
Christmas Morning

The smell of cinnamon and a rich Columbian coffee filled the kitchen. Alexis placed the tray of rolls on the counter. Her hands slightly trembling as she adjusted the cups of coffee. The cozy house of Hazel and Harriet always seemed to glow during the holidays inside and out. Lights Twinkled over every surface. Yet no sparkle of color chased away the heaviness inside her chest.

Hazel appeared from the back room, her hands wiping flour from her apron, eyebrows lifting over the rim of her glasses with a soft smile. "You shouldn't have, dear. Bringing all this on Christmas morning."

Harriet, already settled at the kitchen table with a knit shawl over her shoulders, eyed Alexis with that look that always made her feel like a teenager again.

Harriet muttered under her breath. "She's hiding something." She dropped a spoonful of sugar into her coffee mug. "Isn't that, right?"

Alexis forced a chuckle dropping into the chair beside them. "Can't get anything past you two, can I?"

The tightness in her voice betrayed the lightheartedness she tried to project.

"You don't come by just to bring cinnamon rolls. Hazel reached for a cup of coffee as she sat down. You're saying goodbye, aren't you?"

Alexis shifted. The knot in her stomach tightened. "I just wanted to thank you both. You've been so kind, letting me and Brett help with everything the last couple weeks. But I'm heading back to San Antonio." Her voice wavered, but she steadied it. "It's for the best."

The air in the room thickened. Harriet leaned forward, folding her hands on the table, her eyes sharp, cutting through the pretense. "Is it?"

Alexis blinked. Her back stiffened. "It is. Brett won't change. He's set in his ways. It's like pulling teeth to get him to open up. We're... just not right for each other anymore."

Hazel pushed on her glasses and exchanged a glance with Harriet before she spoke again. "Not right for each other? Or maybe you're just not patient enough?"

The question hit harder than Alexis expected. "What's that supposed to mean?"

"You came here," Harriet began, her gaze unwavering, "to thank us for friendship. That's sweet, but you're really here to convince yourself you're doing the right thing."

Alexis scrunched her nose and scoffed while crossing her arms. "It's not about me. Brett's the one who — "

" — needs to change?" Hazel interrupted. "Or maybe you need to ask yourself if you've changed much either."

Alexis' defenses rose. Frustration bubbled under her skin. "I'm not the one who shuts people out. I'm not the one who'd rather work alone. I'm not the one who doesn't prefer to spend time with —"

"Brett drops everything to help people, doesn't he?" Harriet's words were calm, slicing through Alexis' building protest. "He's always the first to show up when someone needs a hand. He's been doing that for the past twelve days. Maybe he doesn't show it the way you want, but that man likes to be needed."

Alexis opened her mouth to respond, but the words didn't come. Memories of Brett waking up early, staying late, fixing things, lifting things, working beside her without complaint filled her mind. He hadn't exactly embraced every task with enthusiasm, but he hadn't walked away either.

Hazel's hand reached across the table, resting on Alexis' arm. "We've watched you two, dear. He may be quieter, more reserved, but that doesn't mean he doesn't care. You're just expecting him to be someone he's not."

The room, still and warm, seemed to close in on Alexis. Her fingers traced the edge of her coffee cup. Her mind spinning. "But... I can't wait forever. He doesn't... he doesn't show it like I need him to."

Harriet cocked her head. "Do you show him what you need?"

Hazel set down her coffee cup. "Or have you been too busy planning your next event? Are you waiting for him to change without considering you might need to grow with him too?"

Silence pressed between the three women. Alexis shifted in her chair. Her heart raced as the words sank in.

Grow with him?

The phrase echoed in Alexis' head, cutting through every excuse she had clung to. Every frustration she had directed at him suddenly seemed tangled with her own impatience, her own refusal to meet him halfway.

Harriet sighed leaning back in her chair. "You can move on if you want, Alexis. There are plenty of other men out there, ones who might fit the mold you're trying to shove Brett into. But if you're not willing to be patient, to grow together, then maybe you're right — It's time to leave."

The clock on the wall ticked loudly filling the silence in her chest. Realization set in with her throat tightening. She hadn't been patient. She had pushed him away expecting more without giving anything in return.

Hazel stood and moved to the stove to grab another pot of coffee. "Just think about it, darling. Don't rush into something because it feels too hard. Sometimes the hardest things are the ones worth sticking with."

Alexis' phone buzzed against the table, breaking the silence. She picked it up glancing at the screen. Her mouth fell open.

Harriet set down her mug. "Alexis? You, Okay?"

The message glared at Alexis. She chewed on her bottom lip.

"Alexis?"

"Judge says to meet him tomorrow. He's signing the papers."

A tear slid from the corner of her eye. It dropped silently onto her cell phone. She swiped it away quickly, but the knot now forming in her chest twisted tighter.

Hazel's voice, calm, but knowing, floated from the kitchen. "If you leave now, you might regret it. But that's your choice to make."

She stared at the message. Regret. The word lingered, casting a shadow over the decision she'd already made.

Would walking away really make it better? Or am I giving up on something that still had a chance?

The tightness in her chest grew stronger. Her heart kicked out an S.O.S. to her brain.

Stop expecting perfection. Start working for it.

The weight of the last twelve days bore down on her. She chewed on her bottom lip.

He'd tried in his own way, hadn't he?

Quiet, steady, unspoken efforts that she had dismissed because they weren't what she had wanted. But they had been something, and now, maybe, it had come for her turn to try.

Her fingers hovered over her phone. The decision hanging in the balance.

Would she walk away? Or could there be something left to fight for?

FROM: The Whiskey Tattler Editors
TO: Whiskey Tattler Subscribers
CC:
Date: December 25th 10:40 am CST
Subject: You heard it here...anonymously!

THE WHISKEY TATTLER

Anonymous Sources Say...
By Harriet and Hazel Montgomery

Gossip collected from "anonymous" locals a.k.a. Hazel and Harriet for the most part.

Now that the 12 Deeds have concluded and Christmas is near its end, a well-placed "friend" went to the twins' doorstep to whisper that Alexis showed up — red-faced and resigned — to announce she's heading back to San Antonio. She's convinced her marriage is over. Thank goodness we had some sage wisdom for her... but the town gossip doesn't rest.

Here's what our trusted "anonymous" sources are spilling about these last 12 festive days:

"Did you see the milk-crate slides at the grocery store when they tried to chaperone the choir? One kid almost serenaded the cabbage patch instead of Christmas carols — pure chaos!"
— A Christmas Eve cocoa-stand insider

"I heard at the Nativity Debacle™, Mrs. Stapleton nearly dropped the baby Jesus statue — and it may have rolled under the manger.
— An aisle-walking shopper with a flair for dramatics

"Cowboy in those elf stockings? My word—I haven't seen legs like that since the calendar reveal. I got faint just watching!"
— Mrs. Jenkins of Maple Lane, still clutching her mistletoe

"During the present wrapping fiasco, they tied more bows than ribbons... and I swear I saw sparks—almost a near-kiss! But then he whisked off to pour cocoa."
— Local ribbon-shop regular

"They poured over a hundred mint spritzers at the Ball, but he spent more time flirting with Mrs. December than filling glasses."
– A spirited party-goer with a keen eye (and stopwatch)

"When Alexis came by their place... we heard the twins leaned in and said, 'Honey, maybe your husband didn't thaw out — maybe he just gets cold in San Antonio.' Classic Hazel and Harriet
– A generous dinner-party authority

And now, friends, we turn our eyes to Alexis. With 12 Deeds filled with hot cocoa, elf stockings, cowboy charm, nativity disasters, and peppermint-flavored tension, she's decided enough is enough. Yet the twins offered this parting advice:

"Don't hit the road carrying holiday baggage. He showed heat under mistletoe, yes — but also a freezing stare in aisle 3. Trust what chills in January, not the warm glow in December."

Final Thought:
Funny thing — divorce filings spike just after Christmas, thanks to stress, cabin fever, and festive over-indulgence. But the twins reckon Alexis deserves clarity, not anti-ice cleats on broken ice.

Signed with sugar, sass, and too-many-gifts vibes,

Hazel and Harriet Montgomery
Twins, Editors of the Whiskey Tattler, and Whiskey's merry mischief-makers

Chrissy Hartmann

Chapter 18

December 25th
Christmas Late Afternoon
Brett leaned against his kitchen counter. The silence stretched in every direction. In the corner of his cozy kitchen, the lights from a Christmas tree in the corner blinked. Soft shadows from the tree danced across the hardwood floor. His hands absentmindedly traced the edge of his phone — the message he'd sent to inform Alexis — the one telling her Judge Henry would sign the divorce papers on the 26th. He closed his eyes, blew out his breath, and glanced at his phone again. His heart sank. The message remained on the screen with no reply.

But what reply did he expect? Alexis wanted this. Didn't she?

A knock at the door broke his thoughts. Not expecting anyone, Brett's heart kicked. Hope lassoed around his thoughts.

Maybe Alexis had changed her mind. Maybe she came to talk after getting the message. Maybe...

With one push away from the counter, he stood and stepped over to the kitchen door. From a distance he could see a small figure standing out in the dark. Again, hope surged within him. He flung open the door as he hit the switch to the porch light. Chilly air swept into the kitchen.

The light bathed the woman in its glow.

Serena Foster stood there, a wicker basket in her hands smiling softly. "Merry Christmas, Brett,"

Brett's shoulders fell. His chest ached with heaviness immediately. He produced a weak smile and waved Serena into the kitchen. A frown tugged at the corners of his lips as he closed the door.

When he pivoted in his boots, Serena stood at the kitchen counter shaking her head.

Once Brett stepped up to the counter, he slid his phone out of the way. Not sure what to say, he raked a hand through his hair. "What brings you here?"

Serena smiled and shoved the basket toward him. "Brought you something."

Brett held out a hand, stopping the basket from sliding any further. He didn't want anything from her. He didn't need anything from her. In fact, the idea of her being here didn't set well. After all, what if Alexis did show up?

He glanced over at the kitchen window. No one stood on the porch. No extra cars sat in the drive. No one stood waiting for him. Well, no one, but Serena. And she didn't count. They were family. Nothing more. But why had she come?

He held up a hand. "Serena, it's not a good idea for you to be here right now."

"I know, but — "

Brett shook his head. "Please — "

Not waiting for him to finish speaking, she slid the basket toward him again. The scent of fresh steaks and chocolate immediately hit him, stirring up an ache he hadn't realized sat so heavily in his belly. "Thought you might like a little peace offering."

Brett examined the basket, looking at the gift for a beat longer than necessary. A bottle of red wine peeked out of the basket. Two strip steaks were propped alongside of the bottle with a red and white striped box from Beans and Leaves all too famous heart-attack fudge.

"Thanks, but you didn't have to."

Serena's gaze swept over the room. It lingered on the Christmas tree's flickering lights. "Seems like you're not celebrating much this year."

"No reason to." Brett leaned his hands on the back of a chair. His shoulders tense. "Alexis wants the divorce. She's made up her mind."

Serena tilted her head, watching him. With no life in his eyes, it made the defeat obvious. She stepped closer, her voice lowering. "You going to let her go?"

Brett shifted and blew out his breath. "What choice do I have? I'm not what she needs. I can't..." He trailed off, staring at the floor. Silence thickened between them.

Serena crossed her arms. Her eyes never left his. "Can't or won't? Because I've known you forever, Brett. You're loyal, you're steady. You'll show up for anyone who needs help, but when it comes to Alexis, you've built these walls around yourself. Why?"

His jaw clenched. "I'm not like her. I don't need people like she does. I like being alone."

"Do you?"

The question made him flinch on the inside. She stepped forward, tapping a manicured nail on the top of his hand. She leaned closer. "Or is it easier to say you like being alone than admit you're scared to let her in? Because if you really loved being alone, you wouldn't be standing here looking like your whole world's falling apart."

Brett looked up. Their eyes met for the first time. The truth in her words stung more than he wanted to admit. "I don't know how to... be what she needs. She wants me to be more... open, to talk about things."

"And why can't you? She's not asking for the world, right? She's asking to share your life with her, your dreams, your fears, even if they seem small. That's what she wants. You may think she's got it all figured out, but the truth is, she just wants to be included in whatever you've got rattling around in that head of yours."

"I don't have big dreams," Brett muttered, pushing off the counter and pacing the small room. His boots scuffed the floor as he walked, hands on his hips. "I just... I work the ranch. Build things."

She turned resting her back against the countertop. "And what about kids? You ever talk about that with her? Or about maybe opening your own business one day, something bigger than just taking on odd jobs? Because that's the stuff that matters, Brett. Sharing those thoughts, even if they're just ideas. Alexis wants to know she's part of your future, not just someone filling time until it's over."

He stopped pacing. The words sunk in.

Kids? A business?

Not that he cared to admit, but he had thought of those things. But he never brought it up. Not sure why, He'd just never imagined she'd ever want those things, yet at the least discuss them with him. To him, Alexis loved being surrounded by people and better yet people with events. Events she could plan. He couldn't compete with that. Or could he?

Brett started to pace again.

Serena stepped into his path.

He stopped with a brow raised. "What?"

"Stop trying to be something you're not."

On those words, his brow bunched. "Serena?"

"But don't shut her out either. She doesn't need you to be someone else. She needs you to ask her to help you come out of your shell, to be part of your life. That's what love is. It's messy, and it's imperfect, but it's about being vulnerable. You think she doesn't want that with you?"

Frustration raged through his body. His chest tightened. He dragged both hands through his hair about ready to yank it out. He clenched his teeth so not to scream. "I. Don't. Know. If. She. Even. Wants. To. Stay."

Serena scoffed. "Seriously? Let's get real. She wouldn't still be here if she didn't want to be here."

With that statement, Brett stopped pulling on his hair, hair that now looked like a cowlick gone wild.

"And the fact you're even standing here, considering this, means you haven't given up yet either. All you have to do is ask her. Start with that."

His throat tightened. The weight of serena's words wrapped around him. He hadn't given up. But he also hadn't tried to fight for her in the right way. His love had always been quiet, shown through actions rather than words. But maybe it wasn't enough. Maybe she needed to hear it, see it.

"And what if it's too late?"

Serena smiled walking toward the door. "It's never too late. Not if you're willing to fight for it." She paused, glancing back at him. "Call her. Ask her to dinner. Here, tonight." She nodded at the basket and wine. "Show her that you're willing to let her in. You can do that. Can't you?"

Brett stared after her. For a moment, the enormity of the decision washed over him. His heart beat harder, faster, as the reality of what he had to do sunk in. He needed her. He had always needed her, but never let her see that. Could he fix it? His fingers itched toward his phone, the weight of everything pressing down on him.

Serena opened the door and stepped out onto the porch. "Merry Christmas, cuz."

Now standing in the kitchen by himself, he exhaled slowly. The knot in his chest tightening further as he reached for his phone. His thumb hovered over her name, the memory of the last few days flooding back — every small moment, every frustration, every silent plea he hadn't spoken out loud.

Do it, do it now.

His thumb pressed the call button, the ring loud in his ear.

The ringing stopped. She picked up after two rings.

"Alexis. It's me. Come to the ranch." He turned, not sure what to say next when he spotted the basket. "Tonight. I... I've got steaks. And wine. Let's have dinner." The words hung in the air, weighty and uncertain. A pause.

Silence stretched between them. His pulse sped up. His fingers tightened around his phone. "Because." He paused. "I need to talk to you." His heart pounded against his ribcage threatening to bust through. "About... us. Just... come, please."

The silence on the other end allowed the doubt to stir. The fear of rejection crept up his spine. But after a beat, he exhaled, and the corner of his lips curled upward. His shoulders relaxed. The smallest spark of hope ignited in his chest. "Okay. I'll see you at seven."

He hung up. And stood in the quiet house.

Maybe, it's not too late.

FROM: The Whiskey Tattler Editors
TO: Whiskey Tattler Subscribers
CC:
Date: December 25ᵗʰ 4:12 pm CST
Subject: Special Afternoon Update

THE WHISKEY TATTLER

Special Update...
By Harriet and Hazel Montgomery

Happy Holidays from Hazel and Harriet!

This Christmas afternoon, we're back with another festive post. One twin has decided to revisit the cowboy's most memorable romantic misadventures from high school. So, grab some cocoa and enjoy:

Top 5 Times the Cowboy Screwed Up:

Christmas Edition

5. The Mistletoe Misstep
Remember that time in their sophomore year when Brett tried to hang mistletoe in the school hallway, only to have it fall on the principal's head? Not exactly the romantic gesture he intended.

4. The Gift That Wasn't
He once gave his high school sweetheart —AKA Alexis, if you're new to following this blog — a "handmade" necklace for Christmas, which turned out to be from the dollar store. She found the price tag still attached. Oops!

3. The Caroling Catastrophe
Attempting to serenade his crush with Christmas carols, he forgot the lyrics halfway through "Silent Night" and ended up humming the rest. Awkward silence ensued.

2. The Snowball Incident
During a winter date, he playfully threw a snowball at Alexis, but it accidentally hit her in the face. She didn't find it amusing.

1. The Unexpectedly Tender Moment
Despite his blunders, there was that one Christmas Eve when Brett showed up at Alexis' doorstep with a heartfelt apology and a single rose. They spent the evening talking and laughing, making it a night to remember.

Even with all the missteps, it's these moments that make the holidays memorable. Wishing you all a season filled with laughter, love, and a few harmless blunders.

Hazel and Harriet Montgomery

Twins, Editors of the Whiskey Tattler, and Santa's Secret Helpers

Chrissy Hartmann

Chapter 19

December 25th
Christmas Early Evening

The scene unfolded quietly as Alexis arrived at Brett's ranch early Christmas evening. The gravel crunched beneath her boots as she made her way up to the familiar front porch. Her hands clutched the fresh bread tight against her chest. Its warmth seeped through the dish towel. Brett had always preferred quiet nights, and now here they were, about to sit down to dinner after weeks of strained silence. She lingered a moment before knocking, unsure of whatever awaited her inside.

Brett opened the door almost immediately, his tall, toned figure framed by the soft glow of the kitchen light behind him. His expression neutral, but his eyes held something deeper — something between uncertainty and hope. He stepped aside, allowing her to walk in. The scent of roasted vegetables and steak already filled the small ranch house.

"Steaks smell good," she offered, her voice too bright for the tense atmosphere hanging between them.

He didn't respond verbally but nodded, taking the fresh bread from her hands and setting it on the kitchen counter.

Not expecting the dinner to last long, Alexis slipped off her coat and hung it on the hook by the door along with her purse.

The silence stretched as they moved through the small kitchen, the clinking of silverware the only sound breaking the tension. Brett held out the utensils. "Would you do the honor ?" He nodded to the forks, knives, and spoons in his hand. "I usually eat by myself. Not much need to get formal."

A twinge of sadness poked at her heart. Her lips parted, but no words came out. Her eyes shifted to the silverware then to Brett. Not wanting to say the wrong thing, she bit down on her bottom lip and took the silverware. As their fingers touched, a tingle heated her skin.

Brett held on just a moment longer as if he wanted to say something to her, instead he released them. He closed the silverware drawer. Alexis stepped back. Waiting.

Brett pulled plates and glasses from the cabinet.

Alexis shifted her weight from foot to foot as she waited to place each set of the silverware next to the plates. She studied Brett as he placed the dishes on the table. His movements appeared careful, deliberate, like someone trying to avoid any wrong step. The awkwardness hadn't always been between them, only when they'd split, and now? Well, now Alexis wanted to do something about that.

While Brett went about pouring drinks, Alexis took a deep breath. She gazed around the room. The living space hadn't changed much since she left. Still rustic, still bare, with minimal decorations aside from a small wooden nativity she'd brought home years ago that sat on the mantle. The rest of the room seemed exactly as it had been when she left — no sign of her having ever lived there. She swallowed against the ache rising in her throat.

Not sure exactly what to do next, Alexis closed her eyes, took in a breath and slowly let it out. She turned to find Brett watching her. The panic on his face dissipated. Her heart did a little two step. She smiled to herself.

Brett set the bottle of wine down and handed her a glass as she came to the table.

She smiled with a nod.

Brett broke the silence. "So, I've been working on a few ideas. Projects for the house." He released the stem of the glass with their fingers brushing each other's. Another tingle went up Alexis' arm. And as if she had been the only one to feel the tingle, he gestured toward the dining table.

She settled into her chair across from him, arching a brow. "Projects?"

He nodded. Pulling a few sheets of paper from the counter, he spread them across the table — blueprints, scribbled notes in his familiar handwriting. "Figured I could turn the old workshop into something more useful. Maybe an office for you."

Alexis' eyes widened slightly as she stared at the rough plans, his words sinking in. "An office? For me?"

"Yeah," he scratched the back of his neck. "I know you need space to plan all those parties you're always working on. Figured maybe if you had a place here, you wouldn't have to leave the ranch so much."

The words, simple as they were, landed heavily between them. Brett rarely offered anything more than surface conversation, but this... This she could now see him trying. Her heart fluttered unexpectedly.

"I didn't think..." She ran her fingers across the paper. Her voice softer now. "You really put thought into this."

His eyes met hers, a flicker of uncertainty crossing his face. "I should've included you before now. Been too used to doing things my way, on my own. But I can try... If that means you'll stay."

The admission, raw and real, left Alexis frozen for a moment. A part of her had expected this dinner to be another formality, another obligation before the inevitable end. But to her disbelief, he stood in front of her opening up in ways she hadn't expected. She sat up straighter, feeling a crack in her defenses. He never been perfect — she didn't need him to be — but this effort meant something.

"I don't just need space, Brett. I need you to want me here," she said quietly, meeting his gaze. Her voice trembled at the edges, though she fought to keep it steady. "Not just for a room or a project, but for everything."

Brett exhaled, leaning forward, his forearms braced against the table. "I'm trying. Maybe I don't show it the way I should. But I want you here. I just... don't always know how to show it."

Her fingers trembled as they hovered over the plans before she reached across the table, resting her hand on his. The gesture, simple and familiar, grounded them both. She leaned into him. "We're both trying."

Quiet settled over the room again, but this time, not a heavy silence, but a tentative one — hopeful.

She could see the flicker of something in his eyes that she hadn't seen in months — a genuine attempt to bridge the gap between them. "We could make this work." Her thumb traced small circles over his knuckles. "I don't want the divorce either."

Brett's breath hitched, and for the first time that evening, a small, crooked smile tugged at the corner of his mouth. "Then we'll work on it. Together."

Alexis smiled, leaning close enough that the warmth between them became palpable. Her heart pounded as their faces drew nearer. His breath mingled with hers. The space between them grew smaller. Their lips barely touched before the sound of a loud, insistent knock on the door jolted them apart. The moment, fragile as it had been, shattered instantly.

A groan escaped her, half frustration, half disbelief. "Really?" She muttered, glancing at the door as if it were mocking her.

Brett chuckled softly, but the weariness in his expression mirrored her own. He pushed back his chair, shaking his head. "Duty calls, I guess."

Another knock — louder this time — echoed through the room, and Brett's footsteps carried him toward the door. Alexis remained seated, arms crossed as she watched him, her lips pressed into a thin line. Even now, in the middle of everything, someone needed his help.

She growled under her breath. "Just figures."

But she loved that about him, even if it drove her crazy at times. He never hesitated when someone called on him, always reliable, always there for the people who counted on him. And maybe that's part of the problem — he never realized how much she needed him too.

The door creaked open, and Brett's low voice rumbled as he spoke with whoever had come calling.

Alexis sighed, staring down at the blueprint still laid out in front of her. Her gaze softened, tracing the lines and the handwritten notes again. He'd put so much thought into this — more than she had ever given him credit for. Maybe she'd been too quick to judge, too quick to assume he didn't care enough to try.

From the doorway, Brett's voice broke through her reverie. "I'll be right there," he said, turning back to face her. His expression held an apology that went unspoken.

"We'll finish this later," he promised, his tone softer now.

Alexis managed a small smile, nodding in understanding. "Go on, then."

Brett slipped out into the night, the door closing quietly behind him. Alexis sighed again, leaning back in her chair, fingers running absently over the paper once more. This wasn't going to be easy — none of it would be. But for the first time in a long while, she didn't feel quite so alone in trying to make it work.

Reaching for her phone, she glanced at the text message from earlier, the words "Meet the judge tomorrow" glaring back at her. Her stomach twisted at the reminder of the looming decision still hanging over them both. But now... Now they had something to fight for.

Brett's voice echoed in her mind.

I'm trying.

Maybe, just maybe, trying would be enough.

The door creaked open again, and Brett's boots echoed softly across the floor as he reentered the room. He came back to her, to the house they could rebuild together, to the life they still had a chance to save.

"Ready to pick up where we left off?" His face soft in the dim light.

Her heart skipped a beat as she met his gaze. "Yeah, I am."

FROM: The Whiskey Tattler Editors
TO: Whiskey Tattler Subscribers
CC:
BCC:
Date: December 25th 7:45 pm CST
Subject: Christmas Bombshells

THE WHISKEY TATTLER

A Mishmash Update
By Hazel and Harriet Montgomery
Special Holiday Early Evening Update

Hey Whiskey! The grapevine's gone full sleigh-bells over here — And we've got the latest bombshell to drop.

Alexis has been spotted at Brett's home... and for quite a while.
Cue record scratch. In all the years of our inside scoops, this one's got us swirling eggnog in confusion.

What Could This Mean?
Just Friends?
Maybe it's innocent — a holiday gathering, leftovers for dinner, or Brett's air fryer is just that legendary.

Secret Plotting?
Are they co-conspirators in Brett's trademark "Surprise" Holiday Renovation? Could be.
Alexis has impeccable timing.

A Nostalgia-Fueled Rekindle?
High school sweethearts under the mistletoe again? We twins are placing bets on holiday nostalgia.

Soap-Opera Twist Incoming?
Reporters from the Whiskey Gazette better warm up the old flip phones — we smell ratings rising.

Twin Snark Highlights
Whiskey: "We weren't planning to watch a rerun of All My Holidays, but here we are."

"Honestly, if Brett's air fryer is the only reason, we want doorbell cam footage."

"Could it be a gift drop-off? Or is Alexis secretly the elf Brett never knew he needed?"

Phone Poll Results:
Should They Stay Married?
Over holiday calls and FaceTime messaging, we gathered quick, unfiltered opinions from 20 mutual friends:

Option	Votes	%
Stay married (it's nothing)	12	60%
Split them up! Romance rekindled	6	30%
Open Marriage? Let the elf-freedom ring	2	10%

So, hold on to your hat, because from tip to tail, we'll make sure to get the scoop.

Yours in Holiday Spirit,

Hazel and Harriet Montgomery

Twins, Editors of the Whiskey Tattler, and Christmas Truth Seekers

Chrissy Hartmann

Chapter 20

December 25th
Christmas Evening

Brett walked back to Alexis. His skin remained charged from the attempted kiss, an energy that spread through him, chasing away the lingering doubt that had hung between them for months.

She sat at the table, her fingers lightly tracing the rim of her wine glass, the corners of her mouth lifted in a shy smile.

He chuckled softly, a low rumble that came from deep in his chest. "Now where were we?" His voice came out rougher than he intended, his heart pounding in a way that resembled a greenhorn, like a young buck on his first date — like their first date all over again.

Alexis' eyes sparkled as she looked up at him, but before either of them could move, another loud knock shattered the quiet moment, followed by the unmistakable voice of Judge Henry booming from the other side of the door.

"Brett! You in there?"

Another knock echoed, more impatient this time.

Brett's shoulders sagged. He exchanged a look with Alexis. Her raised brow matched the exasperation on his face. They both chuckled despite themselves, though a small part of Brett wanted to ignore the judge's persistent knocking and return to the kiss — or near kiss that had lit the fire between them.

He held up a finger. "One second. Let me take care of this. Don't move."

Brett pivoted and trudged back to the door, swinging it open. "Judge — "

Judge Henry didn't wait for an invitation. The older man bustled inside, brushing off the snow from his coat and stomping his boots on the mat. "Now listen here, I've been thinking about this whole divorce nonsense, and you two — " He halted, his hand halfway through the air in a grand gesture, finally taking in the candle-lit table, the half-empty bottle of wine, and the unmistakable flicker of intimacy in the air.

Alexis stood from the table, her cheeks flushed. The room hummed with the tension of the moment just before the interruption, a tension that Judge Henry either didn't notice or had been too focused on his mission to care about.

"You two..." He repeated, his eyes narrowing as they darted between them. "What's going on here?" His voice had softened, the sharp edge dulling as realization began to dawn on him.

Brett rubbed the back of his neck. His gaze shifted to Alexis before returning to the judge. A small smile crept across his face. "You're too late, Judge."

The older man's eyes widened. "Too late? Too late for what exactly?"

We've worked it out." Brett's words slow but certain. "No divorce. Not anymore. We're going to give this another shot."

Judge Henry stood still for a beat, blinking like he hadn't heard correctly. His mouth opened, then shut. "Well, I'll be..." He stepped closer to the table, eyes scanning the room. "Wine... candles... dinner..." His gaze finally landed on their disheveled appearance, and one of those knowing smirks tugged at the corners of his mouth. "You don't say."

Alexis' laughter bubbled up, soft but genuine, and Brett's grin widened. The judge, who had been pushing them with his stubborn assignments for the last twelve days, finally caught up to the fact that they had beaten him to the finish line.

"I guess I don't need to give you another lecture on love, then," the judge huffed, though his eyes twinkled with amusement. "You two must've been listening all along."

Brett stepped forward, his heart thudding in his chest. The time had come for something more than words, more than promises. "Judge, before you head out, there's something else."

He reached into his pocket, his fingers found the small box he had been carrying around for days, unsure if he would ever have the courage to use it. The weight of it felt different now, lighter, as if this moment had been waiting for him to catch up.

He sank to one knee in front of Alexis.

Alexis gasped, her hand flying to her mouth, her eyes widening in disbelief. "Brett... What are you doing?"

His eyes never left hers, the intensity of everything they had shared in the last few moments — the last few weeks — pouring into his next words. "I've already asked you once, and I haven't done it right since." He opened the small box, revealing a delicate ring, a new one, to add to her wedding band. "But I'm asking again. Alexis, will you stay? Will you give us another chance? Will you be my wife, again, for real this time?"

Alexis' breath hitched, her eyes brimming with unshed tears. Her gaze dropped to the ring, then back up to him. Time seemed to stretch between them, the world narrowing to just this moment. And without hesitation, she knelt in front of him, tears slipping down her cheeks as she laughed softly, her hand trembling as she cupped his cheek. "Yes, Brett. Yes, I will."

He slid the ring onto her finger, his hand surprisingly steady despite the torrent of emotion flooding through him.

She leaned in, capturing his lips with hers in a kiss that spoke of more than just reconciliation — it spoke of hope, of promises renewed, of a future they hadn't given up on.

Judge Henry cleared his throat loudly, but the grin on his face gave him away. He stepped back toward the door, though neither Brett nor Alexis paid him any mind. Their kiss deepened, the warmth between them burning brighter than the candles on the table.

With a chuckle, the judge turned the doorknob, glancing back over his shoulder. "Well, I guess there's nothing more for me to do here."

Brett reluctantly pulled back from Alexis, still kneeling before her, their foreheads resting together as they caught their breath. He grinned at the judge's retreating figure. "Thanks, Judge. Merry Christmas."

The older man winked, slipping out into the night. "I now pronounce you husband and wife," he murmured quietly to himself as he shut the door behind him. He stood on the porch looking out over his quiet small town. The Christmas lights twinkled. The snow fell around him like glitter. He adjusted his hat and smiled to himself.

"Merry Christmas, Whiskey."

Chrissy Hartmann

FROM: The Whiskey Tattler Editors
TO: Whiskey Tattler Subscribers
CC:
Date: December 25th 11:59 pm CST
Subject: What a Christmas!

THE WHISKEY TATTLER

Holiday Finale: All's Well That Ends Well

By Hazel and Harriet Montgomery

After all the holiday hullabaloo, drama, and unexpected gossip, one thing became beautifully clear: no divorce is needed. The judge arrived, reviewed the case, and dropped the final word that sends jingle bells ringing through the hearts of everyone involved.

Judge Henry's parting wisdom:

Out here, a judge's finest work ain't rulings—it's opening folks' eyes to love they still got. My method's simple: I stand aside, and let their hearts do the boot-scooting boogie on over to them branding irons.

So, What's Next?

Second Chance Status:

The couple has officially passed "court-level approval" for reconciliation.

Twins' Verdict:

Hazel and Harriet say: "Let the holiday pie cool before you cut into it, but hey, here's to clean slates!"

Holiday Message:

It's Christmas magic — forgiveness, fresh starts, and a judge-sanctioned "go" to rebuilding what matters most.

From the bottom of our candy-cane hearts, we'd like to say, here's to unexpected reunions, holiday hope, and the gentle art of giving — and receiving — a second chance.

Stay merry—and keep those sleighs rolling forward!

Hazel and Harriet Montgomery

Twins, Editors and Chief of the Whiskey Tattler, and
Antiquers Extraordinaire

THE END

Chrissy Hartmann

Dear Partner,

Well, look at you — finishing this cowboy holiday romance like a champ with marshmallows in your cocoa and a twinkle in your eye.

First off, thank you kindly for moseying into these pages and giving this story a whirl. This was my first time wrangling a cowboy Christmas tale, with *Merry Christmas Whiskey* and let me tell you, it was equal parts joy, chaos, and glitter-frosted madness. Much like an actual holiday with extended family, cow-shaped cookies, and a cowboy who refuses to read instructions. Hmm? No anyone like that? Won't mention any names here, but do have to admit my cowboy looks kinda cute when he throws up those instructions and stomps off.

To be honest, didn't know if I could write such a thing as the year had quite a few rough patches. Lost a father-in-law, a cousin who seemed like a sister to me, and a friend who helped me with *Cherishing Whiskey's Salvation* to a scuba diving accident, then when I thought things were settling down, my cowboy's mamma needed a lot of tending to, then to top it off my own cowboy got real sick, but with a lot of prayers and well wishes, he recovered. Then another project went haywire with the publishing aspect and I broke my foot losing one of my piggies. So in-between my grief, passing out tissues, and keeping the faith, I finally reached the trails end for *Merry Christmas Whiskey*.
And boy howdy was it a blessing.

So, I hope this little slice of Whiskey, Texas gave your heart a warm hug and maybe a few snort-laughs

Chrissy Hartmann

along the way. Writing this story was a ride—full of sass, second chances, and enough holiday spirit to lasso a snowstorm. If you smiled, swooned, or secretly wished you could slow dance in a barn with someone wearing spurs, then I've done my job.
And I'm real grateful, you spent some of your holiday time reading it.

And for a special treat I'd like to share my recipe for the candy cane cream cheese cookies. I've posted the recipe below.
Merry Christmas and Enjoy!

From tip to tail, I thank you kindly!

With all the cowboy love and mistletoe mischief,

Chrissy Hartmann

Candy Cane Cream Cheese Cookies

Serving: 1 cookie

Calories: 120

Carbohydrates: 17

Ingredients:

- 1 cup cold-pressed grapeseed oil

- 8 oz cream cheese

- 1-1/4 cup granulated sugar

- 1 large egg

- 1 teaspoon vanilla extract

- 1/2 teaspoon peppermint extract

- 2-1/2 cups all-purpose flour

- 1 teaspoon baking powder

- 1/2 teaspoon baking soda

- 1/4 teaspoon salt

- 1/2 cup crushed candy canes

Topping – Optional:

- 1/2 cup white chocolate morsals/chips - melted

Chrissy Hartmann

- extra crushed candy canes - For garnish and an extra festive touch.

Instructions:

1. Preheat oven to 350°F (175°C). Line baking sheets with parchment paper to prevent sticking and make cleanup easy.

2. In large mixing bowl, beat softened butter and cream cheese together until light and fluffy. This ensures cookies have a smooth, creamy texture.

3. Gradually mix in the sugar until fully combined. Then, add egg, vanilla extract, and peppermint extract. Continue mixing until smooth.

4. In separate bowl, whisk together flour, baking powder, baking soda, and salt. Gradually add to the wet ingredients, stirring until just combined. Do not overmix, this leads to dense cookies.

5. Gently fold in crushed candy canes for peppermint crunch.

6. Using tablespoon, drop rounded balls of dough onto prepared baking sheets, spacing about 2 inches apart to allow for spreading. Can gently press fork into top of dough to create stripes to fill with sugar sprinkles for candy cane stripe effect.

7. Bake for 10–12 minutes or until the edges are lightly golden and centers are set. Remove from oven and let cookies cool on baking sheet for 5 minutes before transferring to wire rack.

8. Once cookies are slightly cool, if pressed with fork above, sprinkle with green or red sugar sprinkles and extra peppermint or let cookies completely cooled, drizzle with melted white chocolate and sprinkle extra crushed candy canes on top for festive finish.

Leave A Review...

If you've got a minute, I'd be over the moon if you'd leave a review — on Amazon, Goodreads, or wherever you picked up this little nugget of cowboy cheer. Reviews help readers like you find their next feel-good escape and help authors like me keep the stories coming preferably with fewer coffee refills and less yelling at commas.

Thanks again for spending time with Alexis and Brett and the folks of Whiskey.

May your boots stay dry, your cocoa stay hot, and your holiday season stay just wild enough to make good stories later.

Amazon

Good Reads

ABOUT Chrissy Hartmann...

Chrissy Hartmann is a true Buckeye. She's a full-time contemporary western romance author, award-winning short story writer, developmental editor, and book reviewer. She loves all things romance-writing, editing, and reading. Her award-winning short stories are a different vibe, and she's dabbled in poetry too. When not writing, she's sipping coffee, spinning vinyl with her hubby, chilling with her Eagle Scout, and cuddling her fluffballs.
She adores quaint coffee shops, libraries, and indie bookstores. Always up for a writing conference, she's in no rush to grow up with her Muses by her side.

Now out is her 5-star Readers Favorite debut novel, *Rescuing Whiskey's Salvation* and her novella, *Cherishing Whiskey's Salvation*, her cookbook, *The Grub Wrangler: Heartfelt Grapeseed Oil Recipes with Benefits* and her one for the furry friends, *The Grub Wrangler and Gruff: Dog Biscuit Almanac* plus her collection of suspenseful short stories, *Tales from the Prickle Forrest*, and soon to follow *Merry Christmas Whiskey* is her anthology of sweet contemporary western romance short stories, *Buckeye Hearts and Lone Star Kisses*, which will be out next year.

And rolling in next year like a tumbleweed, but hopefully sooner will be her third book of the series, *Treasuring Whiskey's Salvation*.

Not only does Chrissy two-step words across her romances, but she loves creating short stories and blogging for the Prickle Forrest Chronicles ... Vut only when she's not galloping around the countryside with her hubby or son.

For more info, take a gander at https://ChrissyHartmann.com
And don't forget to hitch your wagon to her newsletter at https://PrickleForrestChronicles.com/follow-me
Join the herd and follow her on Goodreads, X, Instagram, and Facebook at USAWriter355.

Now kick off your boots, grab a *Whiskey*, and settle in for some romance where you'll always find cowboy kisses, messy hearts, and small-town sparkle!...

More books by Chrissy...

With writing for over 15 years now, Chrissy Hartmann has written quite the collection of various works, which can all be found on her website, https://chrissyhartmann.com/books and her publisher's website, Prickle Forrest Books, https://prickleforrestbooks.com/book-gallery/

Whiskey Salvation Series:
• Rescuing Whiskey's Salvation - A 5-star Readers' Favorite
• Cherishing Whiskey's Salvation: A Whiskey Salvation Novella
• Merry Christmas Whiskey: A Whiskey Salvation Christmas Novella

Short Stories and Anthologies
• Buckeye Hearts and Lone Star Kisses: Whiskey Salvation Heartland Tales
• Holidays in the Heartland: Ohio Christmas Tales
• Tales from the Prickle Forrest
• Make Christmas Great Again

Cookbooks
• The Grub Wrangler: Heartfelt Grapeseed Oil Recipes with Benefits
• The Grub Wrangler and Gruff: Dog Biscuit Almanac

About Prickle Forrest Books...

Established in 2023, Prickle Forrest Books LLC by Christina H. Benchoff was created due to the stigma attached to self-published and indie authors. Prickle Forrest Books took up the call to help promote these fabulously talented authors to the readers of the world. By doing this, they have provided an affordable service to get the word out. Prickle Forrest Books loves all authors, but Indie and self-published take priority. Prickle Forrest Books hopes one day all authors can publish on a level page. We wish all authors the greatest success in their writing careers. Thank you for letting us help you reach your dreams. For more information contact prickleforrestllc@sssnet.com or visit the website https://prickleforrestbooks.com

Sneak Peek...

Before you go galloping off into the sunset, here's a little taste of my next rodeo: ***Buckeye Hearts and Lone Star Kisses*** — an anthology of short stories packed with sass, smooches, and cowboys who really should know better. Now, I ain't about to go spoiling the whole thing here — cause if I did, you'd have nothing left to read but the copyright page and your own tears. So, kick back, take a gander, and get ready to saddle up for more love, dust, and downright delicious trouble...

Buckeye Hearts and Lone Star Kisses
Whiskey Salvation Heartland Tales

By Chrissy Hartmann

Four stubborn Ohio women. Four smitten Texas cowboys. One state line that don't stand a chance.

The Tyler boys thought they'd wrangled cattle, battled tornadoes, and flown through firestorms — until they crossed into Ohio and met their match. These Buckeye belles don't swoon easy, and sure as boot scooting at midnight, they don't take orders from charm in a cowboy hat. But love has a way of barreling in like a bull at the county fair — loud, messy, and impossible to ignore.

In summer, a stormy island retreat brings one romance author face-to-face with the cowboy she accidentally fell for — and maybe never really knew. In the fall, a cocky Life Flight pilot finds himself grounded by the only nurse in town immune to his high-flying swagger.

In winter, a second-chance cowboy armed with a dog, a rope, and too much frosting makes one last play for the woman who got away.

And in spring, a hot-tempered vineyard princess and a lovestruck cowboy square off over a grape vineyard — and end up neck-deep in grapes and unresolved feelings.

BONUS: Harvest Heart Kisses* —
High school sweethearts reunite when a battered rodeo rider returns home and finds the girl he left behind teaching at the local elementary school — and

tending vines on her family's land. One last ride... or one more chance at forever?

From chili cook-offs to mistletoe ambushes, these seasonal love stories deliver small-town sass, slow-burn chemistry, and cowboy-worthy charm.

Buckeye Hearts and Lone Star Kisses is a clean, feel-good romantic anthology packed with second chances, opposites attract, forced proximity, and small-town hijinks. Perfect for fans of those kind of tales. This exclusive collection includes Harvest Heart Kisses, a bonus second-chance cowboy romance you won't find anywhere else. Saddle up for heart, cowboy smooches, and happily-ever-after — Texas style.